Dance With Me

Rachel Bowdler

Content Warnings

Mentions of weight, with negative experiences of fatphobia and bullying from family members and peers

Body image issues and low self-esteem (developed throughout)

Strong language and injury

Mentions of death and illness

Mild heat level, with one scene of a sexual nature

One

Nora Cassidy had been summoned.

It was barely 8:00 a.m. on a Saturday morning and she had not even the chance to hang her coat by the door when her grandmother's brisk voice penetrated the dance studio like an icy gust of wind. "I wish to speak with you in my office, Nora."

That was never a good sign.

Nora paced the carpeted corridor, wiping her palms of the cold sweat gathering there and tugging at the ends of her scarf. Perhaps if she pulled tight enough, she could strangle herself, pass out, and avoid Constance altogether. There had been worse plans. In fact, she was about to try it when Constance herself emerged from the office with a cold expression. Nora felt herself shrink beneath that cold, gray glare and cast her eyes to the floor. She had grown taller than the old woman years ago, yet Constance still found a way to look down her nose at her — a talent far greater than any other found in Cassidy's School of Dance.

"Is there something on my carpet in need of more urgent attention than what I have to say, child?"

Nora had not been a child in quite some years, yet Constance still managed to make her feel like one every time they held a conversation — which was a rarity these days. Nora tended to save herself the hassle and avoided the old woman like the plague.

She lifted her head and forced her eyes to meet Constance's. "No. I was just about to knock."

"You must stop assuming I have time to waste waiting for you," Constance scolded, standing aside and motioning for Nora to enter. "In."

Nora obeyed, tightening her ponytail self-consciously. Her thick hair had always had a mind of its own — a fact Constance had never appreciated. *Dancers should be well presented. Neat. Elegant. Not have strands of hair flying about all over the shop.* The phantom words still echoed around the stale office.

The blinds had been left closed, though strips of orange sunrise leaked through the gaps and onto the back wall. Seven decades' worth of trophies glinted in the sparse light, won from thousands of different dance competitions. The group photographs to match littered any empty space that could be found among them. Nora could not look at them. She did not want to find her teenage self standing unhappily among her peers, still frozen in one of the most painful times of her life. Sometimes, she wondered why she still came back here to teach at all.

It took her a moment to notice the old television set on top of a cabinet, with a video player beneath. Constance had used the outdated contraption often once, but it had been years since it had last served any purpose, with phones always at hand to playback choreography now. That it had been unearthed from the cobwebbed pits of this place could mean nothing good.

"There is something I have been meaning to talk with you about." Constance brushed past Nora to sit at her desk. It was cluttered with files and bills, unusual for Constance. Normally, everything was neatly stacked away in drawers.

"Okay." Nora remained standing, choosing to ignore the chair that had been pulled out for her. "What is it?"

"I want to show you something first." Constance turned the television on and pressed "play" on the remote, crossing one thin leg over the other and sliding on her rectangular glasses, as though settling herself in for something good. Nora frowned and turned her attention to the screen. It displayed nothing more than an empty stage, a spotlight stamping out the center.

A muffled voice introduced a name she had not heard in a long time — a name she had tried with all her might to forget altogether. *Cassidy's Elite.* Nora's old dance team.

She glimpsed the date flickering in the corner as the dancers emerged from the shadows of the wings.

November 2015.

Her stomach lurched with dread.

"Why are you making me watch this?" A seventeen-year-old Nora appeared, bumbling behind the others, noticeable because she was chubbier and less graceful than the rest of them, especially standing between Sienna Jones and Julian Walker. She was shorter, too, and looked for all the world like she was some misfit who had stumbled onto the stage by accident. She had felt that way, too. Bile rose in her throat.

"No questions until the end." Constance narrowed her eyes in challenge and Nora clamped her mouth shut to prevent further argument.

The music floated out — a song Nora could no longer bring herself to listen to. She chose not to recognize the girl on the screen, whose stomach rolls were visible even from the high angle from which it was filmed. Her thighs rolled as she kicked out her flailing legs. The others beside her were perfect, Julian's leg alignments doing their job well in distracting the audience from the sorry sight beside him. Nora's face flushed with heat, tears pricking her eyes, she looked away in anticipation of the atrocity still to come. A mistake. Constance was surveying her every reaction stonily, her attention a stifling iron hand around her neck that kept her from running away this time.

So Nora kept watching. She watched the girl stumble over Sienna's feet, right into Julian for their next lift. She watched Julian struggle with both the awkward angle she had fallen onto him and her weight. She watched him drop her before they could even hit their next move and send her tumbling straight off the stage, into a black abyss of shadow from which she wished she had never limped back up, even now.

For five years, she had tried to forget the embarrassment she had felt when the music faded, replacing itself with gasps from the audience, and the whispers that had started soon after: "Girls like that weren't fit to dance." "Bless the poor boy who had tried to lift her. Couldn't the teacher see she was too heavy?" "It's a wonder she didn't fall straight through the stage with that weight." "A dancer is supposed to be lean and toned, not the size of an elephant. What did they think would happen?"

For five years, she had failed.

Constance turned the television off. The black screen was far away now, the office a distant thing in which Nora no longer existed. She was still in that ditch beside the stage, listening to them laugh while she cried. She had broken her ankle that day, and the whiplash was still an ache that haunted her sometimes when she slept funny, but the pain had been nothing in comparison to the shame.

"Why did you show me that?" Nora asked through clenched teeth, unable to look her grandmother in the eye.

"I have plans to retire." Constance's voice

was steely, hollow, as she swung her chair back around to Nora and took off her glasses again. She pulled a tissue from the dispenser in front of her and cleaned the lenses absently. "I need to know that I can trust you to take over in my stead."

"Retire?" Nora could only gawp in shock. Constance had been the foundation of this studio long before she had been born. Retirement, even at the age of seventy-seven, was not something Nora had been expecting. "Why?"

"I have spent all of my life here," Constance shrugged. "It's time for a change. Time for some peace."

Nora could not imagine her grandmother sitting by her bay window in her big, expensive house, knitting with a dog on her lap, as most grandmothers did, but she wasn't brave enough to say so aloud. "What makes you think I want to take over?"

"This studio belongs in the family. You're the only one who may inherit it."

Nora loosed a sharp breath and shook her head. "I still don't understand why—"

"I need to know," Constance interrupted impatiently, "that you are capable of taking care of things. I need to know that you are not still the pathetic girl in this video."

"I…" Nora stammered, "I'm not."

It was not a lie. Perhaps watching the video had reminded her of all of the insecurities that had riddled her teenage years, and perhaps she still felt those insecurities gnawing away at her every now and again — when she was shopping for clothes, or when she was here — but she was so much older, braver, more confident than the poor girl on that stage. Her heart ached for that girl, yes, but she also wished she could tell her that she would be okay soon, that it would get better for her.

"And yet," Constance sighed through her teeth, "you don't dance anymore. Haven't, as far as I know, since that competition, with the exception of the lessons you teach."

It wasn't true. Nora still danced, but she danced in private, after Constance left her to lock up the studio and she did not have to worry about anyone watching. When she was free. "Does that really matter?"

"I need a successor who is passionate about dancing — someone who is not just here to open, close, and manage a few classes or hide away in the office to sort out the finances. I need somebody who cares about dance as much as I did and my mother before that. It is no good to me if you do not care about passing on that passion."

"I care about dance," Nora said. "I just… I prefer to teach."

"I know that," Constance nodded tersely, leaning forward on her elbows. Only now did Nora spot how haggard she seemed, her cheeks sunken and her pallid face lined with deep wrinkles. Even her eyes seemed milky in the dim light. "But I need you here more often now, to take over more lessons. I need you to prove to me that you care enough."

"And what if I don't want that?" It was a brave question; her voice trembled as she asked it.

Constance's face hardened. "You would rather pour coffee and live in that shoebox apartment for the rest of your life than carry on your family's legacy?"

"I don't know what I want," she replied, "I wasn't expecting to have to decide first thing this morning."

"There is no decision to make." Constance clasped her knobbly hands together, index fingers pointed together like a blade in Nora's direction. "This studio is yours, and you *will* prove yourself a worthy successor before I hand it over. Your father would have only expected the same."

Her father would have let Nora decide her own path, even if it wasn't the one he wished for her, but Nora was accustomed to keeping silent, even when Constance was wrong. "How long do I have to prepare?"

"It will be a gradual step down, starting next week. I wish for you to have taken over fully by January."

Nora's brows furrowed, stomach twisting. It was already nearing the end of October. "So soon?"

"No need to drag it out." Constance waved a dismissive hand. "I will need you to reduce your hours at the café so that you are available evenings and weekends. You are needed here now. Is that clear?"

Pursing her lips, Nora nodded without commitment. "I'll see what I can do."

A long, frail smile spread itself thin across Constance's wrinkled lips. "I trust you will not disappoint me again, Nora."

Her eyes slid over to the blank television as though in reminder — as though Nora could forget the harsh words that had spewed from Constance's lips that day, as she waited for her X-ray on the hospital ward after the fall. *You have not only embarrassed yourself today, child. You have embarrassed me and every member, past and present, of Cassidy's School of Dance.*

She had always been so harsh, so demeaning, that it was hardly any wonder the fun had been sucked from dancing with others — *for* others — long ago.

It was another thing that Nora did not dare say. Instead, she shuffled out of the office, turning back only once, reluctantly. "I won't."

She had not decided yet if it was the truth.

Two

Julian Walker stretched out his hamstrings at the side of the dance floor, keeping a wary eye on his brother as he folded into his straightened legs. He'd had no idea that Nora Cassidy was the one to teach his lesson, yet there she stood by the mirrors, ruffling his hair as though they were close friends.

Fraser didn't even let Julian ruffle his hair, he noted, not without bitterness. What made her so special?

Her neck was hidden by a knitted beige scarf riddled with holes, she nestled her chin into it as she taught the kids a simple modern dance sequence. It had surprised him just how patient she was — with Fraser in particular. He was prone, sometimes, to causing problems, yet he seemed at ease here. He had even gone to the front of the class to copy Nora's moves, gangly limbs floundering in the mirror's reflection.

Julian hated that he was impressed by it.

He also hated that Sienna was late.

He checked the clock on the wall for a fourth time as he slid into a low lunge with an impatient sigh. His stiff muscles groaned in protest. Being a dancer was twice as hard in the colder months, and he wasn't getting any younger. He looked down, flicking lint picked up off the floor from his knee. When he lifted his head again, he found Nora looming over him with her hands on her hips.

"You're taking up my space."

Julian narrowed his eyes and pulled himself up from the floor as gracefully as his strained body would allow. He'd been overworking himself recently, staying until he was the last one here and then practicing in his small apartment as best he could when he got home. His next audition was in five weeks, and he had to be ready.

"I'm barely on the floor," he said, taking advantage of the fact that he towered well over Nora as he mirrored her scolding stance.

"Your feet were," she countered. "What if one of my kids tripped over them?"

"They're on the other side of the room." He pointed over to where the group were now sliding on their shoes and greeting their parents across the floor. Fraser hovered on the edge of them, casting Julian a timid wave. He flashed his brother a reassuring smile before he turned back to Nora frostily.

"It's not even your lesson today," she huffed, plump lips downturned. "What are you doing here?"

"Not that it's any of your business, but I'm waiting for Sienna," he shot back. "We're rehearsing for the Winter Showcase. You'll be seeing a hell of a lot more of me from now on, so I suggest you put your face straight and get used to it."

At her defiant, bitter scowl, he said, "If we're both lucky and I get this right, you'll be rid of me for good."

"Oh, I definitely am not that lucky," she snapped, green eyes blazing with fire. The intensity of it surprised Julian. They hated each other, yes, but it seemed more intense today — as though he had done something to upset her... something more recent than the incident five years ago, which she still, apparently, had not let go. "Even if Phoenix let you in, they'll soon send you back when they realize you run your mouth more than your feet."

Julian's stomach pooled with ice. Just the sound of the dance company's name sent anxiety shooting through him, and the idea of not getting in... it wasn't an option for him. "Well, Cassidy, at least I have a chance. It's more than I can say for you. Poured anything other than coffee recently? Or is it hot chocolate season now? Sounds riveting, either way."

Nora's expression curled in anger, and Julian suppressed a satisfied smirk. She was just so damn easy to piss off.

"Arrogant prick," she muttered under her breath before walking away. Julian grinned at her retreating figure.

A gust of cool air pried his attention away from her to the door. Sienna stood in the threshold, her nose pink from the cold and her blonde hair tied in its usual immaculate bun. Julian kept his smile up as he approached.

Sienna did not return it.

"Can we talk outside?" She worried at her lip until the clear sheen of her lip gloss dulled, her phone clutched in her hand. Dread hit Julian as he nodded.

"Let me get my shoes."

The smoky, sharp promise of winter lingered in the cool air, though it was still only the end of October. The chill only made Julian feel more uneasy as he followed Sienna around the back of the studio to a small, crumbling half-wall that served as a pathetic barrier from the woods yawning out ahead of them.

Sienna wiped off the moss and dead leaves before sitting on one of the flatter parts of stone, her knee jigging up and down nervously. Julian remained standing, rolling around a stray stone with the toe of his sneakers. "What's this about, S? You know we need to rehearse."

Sienna's bright eyes looked anywhere but at him: the car park beside the studio, the brick wall, the trees guttering with burning reds and golds that fell from the branches with every breath the wind took. It drove Julian crazy. He almost reached out to grip her chin so that she would have to look at him but instead shoved his hands into his coat pockets and pulled at a loose thread until his finger poked through an unravelling hole in the seam.

"The thing is…" she began, gravelly voice wavering as she sniffed, "look, I didn't want to tell you in case I didn't get in, but I auditioned for a school in Edinburgh a few months ago."

Julian stiffened. "Edinburgh?"

Sienna hummed her confirmation, turning to face him finally. A distant sympathy lived on her features, but not much else.

"And now, you're telling me," Julian realized, scratching at the light stubble on his chin, "which means…."

"I got in," she whispered with a nod. "Term starts next week."

"You got in. You're going to Scotland." Julian let out a laugh of disbelief, as bitter as the cold biting at his cheeks. Sienna had never so much as expressed a desire to go to Scotland, let alone move there. "You told me you'd do the duet with me. Phoenix *asked* me for a duet, and I told them to come."

Sienna shrugged helplessly, her hands searching his pockets to tangle with his. They were like ice. "I know. I'm sorry, Julian. I just… I didn't think I'd get in. It was all such short notice."

"No shit," he agreed, pulling his fingers free of her grip and stepping back. "What am I supposed to do now?"

"You'll figure it out. You always do." She squeezed his bicep calmly. Julian could not help but notice there was still no guilt there, in her eyes. Still no apology. Still nothing but a slight unease brought on by his reaction. It wasn't that he didn't want her to go and live out her dreams — but how the hell was he supposed to live out his when she had already promised to help him?

"What about us?" he whispered weakly. They had been together since they were nine-teen. He could not pretend as though his heart was breaking for any other reason than because of where this left him with his duet — when they kissed, fucked, it was not quite the fireworks he knew it should have been — but Sienna was still a big part of his life, and they were good together. Content. They made sense. He had never had to live without her before, as dance partners or as anything else.

"I think some time away would do us good." Sienna swallowed, throat bobbing as she cupped his cheek. "I don't want to be tied down, and I'm sure you don't either. Maybe… maybe we should—"

"You want to break up," he finished bluntly, muscle feathering in his jaw.

"Yes," Sienna answered. "Is that okay?"

Julian scoffed. "Do I get a say? Sounds to me as though you've already made your mind up."

"I'm as surprised by this as you."

"I don't think so." Julian sighed and pulled her hands away patiently. He couldn't look at her a moment longer. If he did, he might not be able to leave her at all. "Good luck in Edinburgh, Sienna."

"Julian—" Sienna's plea was hollow, a waste of breath — one that Julian had no interest in hearing. He had to figure out something for the Winter Showcase. The callback audition, he could do alone, but he had already told the director of the company that he had a duet planned for the show, and Jennifer Phoenix herself had vowed to come to his dead-end town just to see him. She didn't do that for just anyone.

He had to figure it out. Now.

He expected the studio to be empty when he walked back in — the lights were turned off, bathing the room in an indigo twilight and reflecting distorted silhouettes in the mirrors — but it wasn't. Soft music scattered across the floor, and she, with it.

Nora Cassidy, dancing. He hadn't seen that in a long, long time.

He stepped out before she caught sight of him, peering through the window instead. She wasn't bad at all, though he could tell by the frequent stops and starts that she was only improvising. Even so, she still had it in her, her body gliding across the floor as she arched and leaped, spun and jolted. Her copper hair had come loose of its tie, falling about her face as she curled her body into new shapes that he was unable to imagine in his own dances. Her body carried the rhythm through her bones, through splayed fingers and pointed toes, freezing and melting with the melody so that Julian could do nothing but hold his breath and wait for the next drop, the next beat, both in his chest and in her.

A lot better than "not bad," then. Surprisingly, much, much better than he had ever seen her before — as though she had succumbed to the music, let it take her body hostage and fling her about in waves. And he could feel it. Everything she felt, he could feel, too.

He stepped back, heart hammering against his rib cage. When was the last time he had danced that way just because he could? He had been rigid in his own bones recently, lost to the well-planned choreography and the same tired moves he'd been doing since he was an eight-year-old beginner.

He did not notice the old woman standing behind him until he fell back and almost stood on her foot. Constance Cassidy didn't so much as flinch, though he was twice her size and probably could have crushed her fragile bones — not that he'd dare step a hair out of line with her.

She peered up at him over her glasses, lips pursed into a fine line.

"Did you know that your granddaughter was still dancing?" he asked in disbelief, pointing over his shoulder to the dark dance studio. Behind her, he glimpsed Fraser waiting by the car and cast him a patient wave to let him know he'd be there in a moment. With everything that had just happened, Julian had forgotten he was even here and

17

immediately felt guilty for it.

"No," Constance replied. "I didn't. The revelation was one of the few things still capable of surprising me. Another one would be Miss Sienna leaving you high and dry for your audition."

Julian frowned, taken aback.

Constance tapped her crooked nose knowingly. "If you wish for private conversations, Mr. Walker, perhaps choose somewhere further from my office."

He eased in understanding. Of course. The wall was just below Constance's window, and though it had been closed, he wouldn't put it past the wily old woman to find a way around it.

"It sounds like you're in some hot water," she continued and did not seem sorry to say it. Her lips curled into a pleased smile, which only made Julian more wary.

"It's not ideal," he admitted, brows knitted together so tightly he could practically feel the shadows from them cast across his eyes.

"It is a good thing, then," Constance said, "that I have a solution for you. Would you like to hear it?"

Julian might have gotten on his knees and begged if it meant saving his audition. Instead, he only nodded and let Constance propose her idea in his ear.

Three

Nora sighed wistfully as she leaned across the counter, fingers dancing across the smooth surface she had just wiped down. It was the café's lethargic hour between breakfast and lunch, where she did not have much to do but clean down the coffee machines and serve the odd customer who had nowhere better to be on a weekday. That day, there was none. The café was dead, save for her and Annie, who slid a mug of hot chocolate over and sat on the stool opposite, as though she was a customer herself rather than the owner.

"Have you got anything stronger?" Nora only half joked as she blew gently on the steam, cradling the warm mug in her hands.

"So your grandmother just expects you to drop everything to take over the dance studio?" Annie confirmed as she sipped her own coffee. Her short hair flicked out in every direction thanks to the rain shattering incessantly on the concrete outside, turning everything past the bright orange Halloween pumpkin stickers in the window a dull grey. There was nowhere that Nora would rather be than here on days like this — not even her own apartment. The rich smell of coffee beans and her best friend/boss' presence was more a comfort than anything else in her life. To think that if she really did take over the studio, she would lose these moments.

"Correct," Nora nodded with a grimace. "She can't comprehend that I might have other career plans."

Annie raised an eyebrow. "Do you?"

"Well, no," she replied. "But that's beside the point. I could have."

"Can I offer my two cents?"

"No," Nora said bluntly, "because your two cents are always completely rational, and I'd much rather stew in all of my anger and confusion."

"Nora, you're almost twenty-three years old," Annie continued anyway, pushing away her mug to show that Nora had her undivided attention. She was good at that, Annie, with her soft, sympathetic doe eyes that were always unafraid to lock another person's in their firm grasp. Nora was always the first one to squirm away. "You're not a child anymore, and that means she can't control you. Not really. If you don't want the studio, don't take it."

Nora blinked expectantly. "I'm sensing a 'but.'"

"*But*," Annie offered, "I think there's a reason you haven't pursued anything else. I think you've been waiting for this, on some level. You always knew it would be yours eventually."

"Not this soon."

"Maybe this is a good time for it. You're getting a little too content with letting me take advantage of the fact that I'm your boss as well as your best friend. You work more hours here than I do."

"I like it here." Nora pouted, searching the hot chocolate for marshmallows with her spoon so she wouldn't have to face what Annie was saying.

Sensing it, Annie pulled the spoon out of her hand as though she were a misbehaving child. She would make a wonderful mother one day. Nora had always thought so, but it was made clear in moments like these.

"You feel safe here. It's not the same. And as much as I like having you around all the time, don't you think it's time to create your own safe space?"

"In the dance studio?" Nora scoffed. "Where I spent my adolescence hating myself and getting teased constantly?"

"That was then," Annie said. "You could change it completely. Make sure the kids there now never have to go through what you went through. You could make a real difference if you wanted to. Make dancing fun again."

Nora narrowed her eyes, though she knew Annie was right. It had always been a dream to help kids who struggled through dance — a pipe dream, perhaps, but still a dream. She had seen some of her students light up in her lessons and it left her feeling warm, proud. The café was her haven, but teaching was where she felt best about herself, even if it was in the same place that broke her.

"Besides, what will happen to it otherwise?" A sneer curled across Annie's lips as she picked up her mug and sipped again: a signal that the serious part of the conversation was over, thank heaven. "Some prat like Julian Walker will get it, even though he couldn't care less about anyone but himself, and he'll run it to the ground."

Nora hummed pensively and resumed slouching over her drink.

"All I'm saying is you could make it into something different — something better. Aren't you the least bit tempted to do away with those old traditions and attitudes and create a space for kids to just do what they love without all of the nastiness and pressure?"

"I think you're just trying to get rid of me," Nora retorted.

"Well, that would just be a bonus." Annie smirked, though her hand found Nora's again and squeezed. It was warm, comforting, familiar. Annie was the only real friend — family, even — that Nora had, and she appreciated her more than she could ever tell her. "Just think about it."

"I will," she agreed with a small smile. "Promise."

The tinkle of the bell above the door caused Nora to straighten, only to sag in disgust a moment later when Julian Walker walked in, shielding himself from the rain with his hood. His coat was dripping wet and the excess pooled by his feet. Nora huffed and pulled out the mop from the cupboard behind the counter before she even thought about asking why he was here.

"What do you want?" She jabbed the mop around his feet to shoo him away from the slippery tiles.

"Your customer service is shocking," he noted in that cocky little voice that Nora despised. "I would fire her if I were you, Miss Lewis."

Annie only scowled at him with her mug tilted to her lips. "That's my cue to go. I'll be back before lunch."

A mangled gasp of betrayal caught in Nora's throat as Annie weaved around her and the mop, pulling on her raincoat before she submerged herself in the torrent outside. *I hope she catches a cold, the traitor,* Nora thought scornfully.

"What do you want?" she repeated through gritted teeth, attacking the tiles furiously with the twisted strings of the mophead until the floor shone beneath the fluorescents.

Julian pulled down his hood and raked his sopping hair off his face. Droplets still rolled from his head, his eyelashes, his nose, stopping at his mouth, where his tongue caught them. "I came to make you an offer."

Nora wrinkled her nose with derision and thrust the mop to one side. "My answer is no."

The corner of Julian's mouth twitched in amusement. "You haven't even heard what it is yet."

"I don't need to," Nora deadpanned, crossing her arms over her chest resolutely. "No."

"Oh, come on, Cassidy. Isn't it time we put this little war aside and worked together?"

Nora raised an eyebrow. "Is this about the studio?"

His smug expression turned bewildered. "What about the studio?"

"Let me guess: You caught wind of my grandmother's retirement, and you want to take it off my hands."

"Quite the conspiracy theory." His thick brows knitted together. "But you're wrong. I had no idea, actually."

Nora tried to hide her surprise as she put away the mop — though she would need it again when he left, and perhaps before then, if he pissed her off enough to warrant using the wooden end as a weapon. "Alright then, I'll humor you. What's the offer?"

"Be my dance partner for the Winter Showcase."

He said it so gravely, without any of his usual mocking or crooked grin, that Nora filled the void herself by letting out a high-pitched laugh. "Yeah. Sure."

"I'm serious."

Nora wandered behind the counter, piling and re-piling the serviettes with uncertain hands. She was quickly beginning to tire of his presence.

"I don't know what game you're playing, Julian, but my answer is no. Are you done?"

His jaw tightened in frustration as he pressed his palms into the wooden surface. "This isn't a game." His voice had lowered to a mutter, shadows darkening his face. "I need a dance partner, and you're the only one there is."

"And what happened to your girlfriend?"

"She's leaving for Edinburgh tomorrow. She's moving there."

Something in his tone was somber enough that Nora faltered. She lifted her gaze, scrutinizing him for a moment. His smirk had still not returned. His entire body seemed taut with stress. Every corded muscle rippling beneath his jacket, every movement — every blink, even — shook with tension, as though he was a string being pulled too tightly and just about ready to snap.

"There's no one else, Nora." His brown almond eyes gleamed with unspoken pleas. "Not one other person in this town who can dance with me the way you can or knows how to choreograph for my skill set. I've seen you teach my brother. I know you can help me. Please."

Nora opened her mouth to respond, but her throat only produced a strangled noise. Weakness gnawed at her for only a moment, but it was enough to make her forget how much she hated the man in front of her, enough to make her want to help him. And then she remembered, thought of what it was he was asking of her, and her eyes shuttered. "I don't dance anymore."

"Yes, you do." He caught her wrist across the counter before she could walk away, his icy thumb and finger pinching her flesh gently. She glanced down at the touch, half in shock and half in disdain. "I see you. When you think everyone is gone, I see you — and I see your choreography. Even when you're improvising, you throw moves in there I would never have thought to try. I need you, Nora."

Embarrassment coiled in Nora's stomach at the thought of her most private moments being watched — by *him*. It made her want to claw off her skin and find a new one to wear. She tried to ignore it as she pulled out of his grasp.

"I'm sorry, you what?" Nora cupped her hand to her ear, wanting to hear him say the last part again. Let him be the one to lose his dignity and pride for once.

"I need you," he ground out through his teeth. It was clear how much he loathed saying it.

"You need me." Nora pretended to ponder it, dragging out the moment by pulling the pen from her apron and tapping it against her chin. She hummed dramatically, reveling in the way that he shifted from foot to foot in impatience. And then, when she had drained all the enjoyment she could get out of his discomfort, she said: "Tempting, really. But no."

"Nora—"

"I'm sorry about Sienna, Julian," she said,

though nothing about her tone sounded sorry even to her own ears, "but I can't help you."

"You don't understand," he countered. "The showcase is half of my audition, and I promised Jennifer Phoenix herself that I'd be doing a duet. They've already seen me as a soloist. They need more. They need something exceptional."

"Sounds like your problem, not mine," Nora replied, so coldly she surprised even herself. But she couldn't help it. She couldn't help but remember Julian's hands losing their grip on her waist, the way his feet had tangled with hers and sent her flying off that stage — and he hadn't even tried to help. He'd just stood over her with the rest of them, watching as tears pricked her eyes. She'd lost the last shard of her old self that day. She wouldn't be a fool and go back to that now.

"If I don't do this, Cassidy, I won't get in. I don't have any other options."

Nora shrugged. "Then you don't have any options."

Julian rocked back on his heel, letting her words resonate in the quiet of the café for a moment before he shook his head, lips pursed sourly. "You can't hold what happened that day against me forever."

Her stomach twisted at the mention of it.

"I can certainly try," she forced out. "I don't owe you anything, Julian. Remember that before you ask anything of me again."

He nodded in defeat, patting the counter before he sauntered off with his shoulders squared. "I'm sure you'll have no trouble reminding me, Cassidy."

She gulped down the guilt she felt at his crestfallen expression. She had never seen him so resigned, so hopeless. But she couldn't dance. *Wouldn't* dance. Not with him, and not with anyone else.

So she let him leave, watching as he pulled his hood over his head before surrendering himself to the miserable weather.

Nora had expected to feel satisfied after finally one-upping Julian. Instead, she just felt awful and cold.

In fact, she felt just like her grandmother.

Four

Nora was untying her shoes — reluctantly, given that the rain had soaked through her socks and turned her toes into blocks of ice — when her grandmother cornered her that afternoon with a slip of paper.

"What's this?" Nora arched an eyebrow as she kicked off her trainers and took the sheet. It was full of grids and times, color-coded and labeled with days of the week. A schedule much like the ones Constance had forced her to keep as a child. Just looking at it made her shudder inwardly.

"I took the liberty of making you a weekly rehearsal schedule," Constance responded with a proud sniff. "I'd like very much for you to keep to it."

"Constance," Nora sighed impatiently, "I have a job. I can't just drop everything—"

"If you take over this studio, child, you will no longer need worry about that little shack you call a café," Constance interrupted, face lined with sternness. "This is your priority now."

Nora rolled her eyes as inconspicuously as she could, peering down at the grid. Every evening was filled in with lessons she would be taking over from Constance, along with the few a week she already taught. Her weekends, too, were shaded a vile green to signal jazz, modern, baby ballet, stamina, and technique. White blocks were interspersed throughout — breaks, hopefully, but that did not seem like Constance.

"What's the white?"

"Your rehearsals with Julian, of course."

"No, Constance—"

"Do not 'no, Constance' me." Her knobbly finger jutted into Nora's sternum like an extra collarbone. "I told you you would need to prove yourself. You can start with a performance at the Winter Showcase."

A lump formed in Nora's throat at the very idea. The only thing that kept her from shouting, *pleading*, was the fact that her students were arriving for their beginner's class and they were all far too young to be subjected to the obscenities floating around Nora's tongue.

"I can't do that," she whispered helplessly. "You know I can't."

"'Can't' is not a word. Not in this studio." Constance gestured to the quote printed in black on the white brick wall behind them. It had always served as more of a threat than a source of inspiration for the students, used whenever Nora could not master a move and Constance insisted she tried again. She had pulled many a muscle and sustained many an injury because of that blasted sign. If she *did* wind up taking over, it would be the first thing to go. "You will do this for me, Nora, and you will do it for the studio. I don't care about your personal vendetta against Mr. Walker or your cowardice when it comes to performing. A director of an international company is coming to this show, and we will give her what she expects to see."

Nora swallowed down her bile. "The last time I danced with Julian, he dropped me in front of everyone."

"And whose fault was that? You told me you are no longer the girl who fell off the stage and decided never to perform again. Show me that is true, and the studio is yours."

Nora sucked in a sharp breath. She could walk away now, refuse her inheritance, and never think about dance again. Never feel that embarrassment and unworthiness live in her like a wolf licking her insides with a tongue like sandpaper. But then what? Annie had been right. Nora loved teaching, and she wanted to make this place better than it had been for her.

She couldn't just walk away.

She searched for something to focus on desperately and found a dozen pairs of innocent eyes on her as they waited patiently to be summoned to the dance floor. Their parents sat behind them with wide, proud grins. For some of them, this was the highlight of their week. Their days would not get any better than entering these four mirrored walls and they relied on her to help.

Her father had wanted this for her, too. She could feel his presence, still, beneath the silver reflections and hidden in the brickwork. The soles of his feet had padded against the wooden floorboards long before her own. It was one of the reasons she still danced, even now: to feel him. To be with him again. To let him know she wouldn't give up on a dream they had once shared — a dream that had almost shattered after his passing but still, somehow, was held together with superglue.

"I'll try," Nora promised finally.

"Trying is not good enough here," Constance countered, chin jutting in the air. She tapped her foot, knowing that those around them were watching and probably enjoying every moment. She had always taken too much joy in scolding; knowing she could still do it to Nora must have given her another rush of power. "Tell me that you will."

"I will," Nora sighed grimly, folding up the piece of paper and tucking it away in her bag.

"Good. Your first rehearsal with Mr. Walker is tomorrow. I expect there will be no problems."

"There'll be no problems." Even as Nora said it, her blood began to boil hot enough to blister. She forced a confident smile to her face anyway. *I am not that girl anymore*, she thought, a mantra she kept repeating in her head. "I promise."

∞ ∞ ∞

There was a peace that came with dancing in the dark, when everyone else had gone home and Nora was the only one left. It was something she had done for years, when she had finally been gifted a second set of keys from her grandmother. Her feet seemed to glide more freely across the floorboards, and her arms felt less constricted in the vast space and shadows. She could feel her father, watching. Smiling.

Sometimes, she didn't even need music. That night was one of those nights. The thoughts in her head were quite enough to listen to, dance to, until an arrogant drawl caused her to falter.

"Well, look what we have here."

She flashed her eyes to the mirror, already knowing who she would find: Julian leaned against the doorframe, his arms crossed over his broad chest. She couldn't see his expression in the shadows, but she could hear his smirk in the way he clicked his tongue. "Nora Cassidy, dancing. But that can't be right, can it? Nora doesn't dance anymore. She told me so only this morning."

"Nora could quite easily punch you in the face, if you would prefer." She thanked the heavens that it was dark and he was less likely to see her cheeks burning in her reflection.

Julian took a step and then another toward

her, boots squeaking across the dance floor until he was directly behind her. Still, she did not turn around. "Is that a promise, Cassidy?"

"How did you even get in here?" she spat. "I locked up."

He dangled a spare set of keys in front of her face. She turned to face him then, if only so he could catch her rolling eyes.

"Of course. You're so far up my grandmother's ass that she's probably choking on your hair gel."

He chuckled, but it came out as more of a growl. "How long did it take you to think up that one?"

"Not all of us spend all day practicing our insults in a mirror, Julian." She huffed and turned on her heel, collecting her bag from the side of the floor. "You're lucky I'm here for you tonight."

"Oh?" He slanted his head, lined shadows slithering across his face where the streetlights poured in through the window. "You'd be surprised how often I hear that. Can't say I was expecting it from you, though."

"Since you and my grandmother are such good chums these days, I expect she's already told you I'm doing the duet." Nora pulled a sheet of paper from her bag — this one, not folded or crumpled, like her own.

"She didn't mention it, actually." His voice lifted in surprise. "She did propose I ask you in the first place. Didn't think you'd go for it, though. I'm glad you came around, Cassidy."

"I'm not doing this for you," Nora bit back, thrusting the paper into his hands. "I'm doing this for her and for the studio... and I'm doing it for myself. Is that clear?"

"Crystal." He flashed his teeth. "What's this?"

"A copy of my schedule — another gift from Constance. If you want to do this, we'll do it properly. As you can see, I'm busy teaching most days, so don't waste any more of my time by being late."

"Wouldn't dream of it."

That lazy smirk was making her skin crawl now, even if it was shrouded by darkness. She huffed to keep her anger at bay and pulled on her coat and scarf.

"Good. Then I'll see you tomorrow evening at six."

"You certainly will, partner," he nodded, condescension seeping into his words. "Six on the dot. No time wasting."

"Don't call me 'partner,'" she muttered, already walking away along the strip of moonlight leading to the door. "This isn't a cowboy movie."

"Nora?"

Nora turned, sweeping her hair from her scarf. She squinted, spotting something in Julian's face she had not been expecting... something that looked an awful lot like vulnerability. It might have been a trick of the light, but it didn't feel that way when he said his next words.

"Thank you. You're doing me a real favor here."

"Like I said," she replied coldly, the brisk night air blowing in as she opened the door, "I'm not doing it for you."

She left Julian in the darkness and hoped that, by some miracle, he would not be waiting for her tomorrow evening.

Nora knew, though, that she was not that lucky.

Five

Nora checked the clock above the wall of mirrors when Julian sauntered into the studio the next day: six on the dot, as promised. She did not show her pleasant surprise as she peeled off her socks and dropped into a lunge to warm up. The studio was cold, so she kept her scarf and jacket on as she switched legs.

"Are you ready, Cassidy?" Julian questioned, bravely pulling off his own coat and shoes before joining her on the floor.

"No," she replied bluntly. "Have you chosen a song?"

"You really don't waste your time, do you? Are you that eager to dance with me?" He cocked his head and stood, plugging his phone into the speakers in the corner. The dance studio was dead. It was Halloween, and class attendance had been sparse, so with the permission of the parents, Nora had dismissed the kids early to go trick or treating. Even Constance wasn't in her office that night, though she hardly thought her grandmother would be celebrating. She didn't need to dress up anyway. She was terrifying enough without costume. "I couldn't choose between the two of them.

37

Figured you might be able to help."

"Already getting me to do the heavy lifting?" Nora retorted but listened anyway as the first song began to play. It was a familiar one by The Cinematic Orchestra. She had seen a lot of people choreograph to it before, both here and online. "Play me the other option."

"Yes, ma'am," he obeyed and changed the song. This one had more depth to it in the harmonies and instruments, with moments of pause she could imagine matching with her body. There was still something missing, though.

"What do you want this to be about? Are we choreographing to a narrative?"

Julian hesitated, turning the music down until the lyrics were nothing more than a whisper. "The narrative is the story of how I am so wonderfully talented that Jennifer Phoenix instantly accepts me into her company."

"I'm not a miracle worker." Nora couldn't help the snarky response. They had been at one another's throats for so many years that it came as naturally to her as breathing now. Julian only shot her a scathing scowl and stopped the music altogether. "I mean, are you going to tell a story, or is this just some dance you think you can breeze through without emotion?"

"I'm sensing that there's a right answer here."

"And I'm sensing that if you were being honest, you wouldn't pick it." She shoved him out of the way and plugged her own phone in, pulling up her Spotify. "If you want to stand out, you can't just dance to the same tired songs with the same moves and style as everyone else. You need a story to tell, a reason to be on that stage other than just to impress Phoenix."

Julian pressed his lips into a thin line, ready to argue when Nora played the song she had in mind. It was an instrumental that had been on repeat for weeks. She'd been dancing to it in the shower, in her apartment, and in the café. When she couldn't let the moves out, she trapped them in her head for later. It felt oddly personal to play it in front of him now, but she had saved it for a reason. It told a story — a story she wanted to tell, too — of heartbreak and loneliness, loss and pain, breaking and healing.

Julian nodded his head in time to the piano melody, knees bending as though he was ready to take off. "Okay. Not bad, Cassidy. I'll let you have this one."

"So kind of you." Sarcasm laced her words as she paused the music again and led him into the center of the floor. She shrugged off her jacket and pulled her thick hair up into a bun, fighting the habit to look past her reflection and instead gauging her own appearance just for a moment. She still did not have a dancer's body — far from it.

"Are you finished playing with your hair?" Julian asked impatiently.

Nora only glared and gestured to the space

in front of her. "It's your dance. Lead the way."

He did, settling into his role well. Nora felt out of sorts at first, the movements not coming quite as naturally to her as they once had. They managed the beginning sequence, though, with Julian starting in the center and Nora weaving around him until they fell into unison. They'd figured out the first few bars within the hour, and there were surprisingly fewer arguments than had been expected. Only short bickering interspersed the dance until Nora set off on the wrong foot. Julian huffed to stop the music, raking back his hair. It had fallen across his eyes with all the moving around, taking on a life of its own. Nora's wasn't much better.

"You're holding back on me," he accused, slamming down his phone.

Nora frowned, loosing a ragged breath. Her cheeks were rosy, a light sheen of sweat coating her face. "No, I'm not."

"Yes, you are," he scolded. "You're not always this shit."

"Excuse me?" The words, like a dagger through her stomach, ignited an anger that had almost been lost to the music a few moments ago.

"I saw you improv the other night. You put your heart into it. Now, you're like dead weight."

Another pang through her stomach, this time shooting up to her chest. "I'm still getting the hang of the choreography. Give me a chance."

A muscle in Julian's jaw quivered in irritation. "I'm not playing around here, Cassidy. I need you to at least *try*."

"I *am* trying," she bit back, hands curling into fists so tightly she could feel her nails embedding themselves in her clammy palms. "If I'm not good enough, Julian, you're welcome to find someone else."

She was already slipping on her trainers haphazardly and then, without tying the laces, collected her coat and wound her scarf back around her neck. "You're so ungrateful. You know, I have better ways to spend my evenings than with you. I didn't have to be here."

Julian still stood in the same spot, his body hewn from rich brown stone. "No? Did Constance give you permission to take the night off?"

"What?"

His eyebrows twitched with gratification. He still loved getting under her skin. *Dick.* "Well, she controls everything else in your life, doesn't she?"

"Oh, fuck you, Julian," she managed to breathe out through clenched teeth, marching toward the door as elegantly as she could with shoes that were only half on her feet.

"Go on, do what Nora Cassidy does best," he called behind her. "Give up as soon as it gets tough."

Nora whipped around, her face so hot she wouldn't have been surprised if plumes of smoke curled around the edge of her vision. "Well, you always had a talent for chasing me as far away from you as possible." Her hand was already on the door handle before he spoke, but she realized the door was locked and the keys were in her bag by the mirrors.

"You can't blame me for every negative thing in your life."

"I can certainly try," she snapped, pulling on the door, though she knew it would be in vain. "You can go to hell. You *and* your duet. I'm not doing it."

His face was all harsh lines and high cheekbones, squared jaw and rigid muscles. The veins protruding from his arms looked as though they might pop at any moment. *Good*, Nora thought. She'd happily clean his remains up from the floor. She kept her head held high as she funneled back to her bag and hauled it onto her shoulder, rooting through her belongings until she found the keys jangling against the silk lining at the bottom.

Julian deflated in her periphery, a ragged breath escaping his lips as he looked up at the ceiling. Nora wanted to tell him that nobody up there in the heavens would be willing to help a bastard like him.

"Alright." He spoke calmly now, though a dark hint of rage remained. "You've made your point."

"I'm not making a point," she replied, going back to the door and unlocking it. "I'm leaving. Lock up when you're done being a prick."

"Nora." It wasn't often he used her first name. It was enough for her grip to falter and, as though feeding off her weakness, he was there a moment later, keeping the door shut tight in its frame with his hand. "I need you for this duet. You know I do."

"Do you?" Nora arched an eyebrow. "I thought I was a dead weight."

Julian inhaled steadily, eyes fluttering shut for a second. For once, he seemed more uncomfortable than Nora, and she took joy in that, at least. "You're right. You need time to adjust to the choreography. I wasn't being fair."

She tried to pull the door open, but he slammed it shut again. "Please," he pleaded, brown eyes swirling with desperation. "I'm just... I'm stressed, okay? I need to get accepted into Phoenix. I can't stay here. The pressure is making me lose my head a bit. Don't give up yet. Please."

His throat bobbed as though it pained him to say it. There was enough vulnerability etched into his expression that Nora softened and dropped her hands from the door.

"I won't put up with your bullshit," she warned. "If you talk to me like that again, we're done. I'm not a sweet little teenager anymore, and you won't talk down to me like I am."

"You were never a sweet little teenager," he countered, but his features had smoothed. "But you're right. It won't happen again."

"No," she agreed icily, "it won't."

"Let's just call it a night. We'll start again tomorrow."

"Can't wait," she deadpanned, and then she weaved behind him again to open the door. The air was damp with low-lying mist, dead leaves piled in a soggy heap by the door. She stepped through them, not caring if they dirtied her shoes. She just needed to get out before it got to be too much. Before she fell back to the place she had vowed never to go again.

Before Julian Walker broke everything she had strengthened in herself these last few years.

Six

It was too early. November had brought with it a chill that pierced right through Nora's fleece thermals to her very bones, her teeth chattered as she put her keys in the door, only to find the studio already unlocked.

Her hands curled around the phone in her pocket instinctively, worried that perhaps somebody had broken in somehow, but then she saw that Julian was already slick with sweat and leaping around the place in only a tank top and leggings and relaxed only slightly. She might have preferred an intruder to the sight of his face, lined with concentration, this early in the morning. No music played, though he was dancing, his breaths falling out of him with each movement and his bare feet padding across the floors.

If she didn't hate him so much, she might have thought him beautiful. His lean muscles made him an elegant dancer, able to twist himself any way he pleased, leap high enough to touch the old disco ball hanging from the ceiling, and make it all look effortless in the process. She recognized some of the choreography from the sequence they had figured out last night. As he fell into a pirouette, his eyes locked on hers and he came to a halt.

"Did you sleep here?" she grumbled, shutting out the cold quickly and hanging her bag on the hook. She did not dare part with her coat or scarf yet.

"Might as well have," he replied, scratching his neck uncomfortably. Perhaps he was wondering if she was still mad — not that it would make a difference, what with the ungodly hour, the fact she had not had her morning cup of coffee yet, and of course, her eternal disdain for Julian.

"You're chirpy."

"Don't talk to me this early unless you want your head bitten off." She stifled a yawn with her hand and pulled out her schedule. She was teaching a small group of lyrical dancers this morning, most of them teens. Better than hyperactive kids, she supposed.

"As opposed to the usual, when you're so kind and gentle toward me?" He picked up his water and slumped onto the floor as he took a sip. "What are you doing here anyway? We're not rehearsing until eleven."

"Teaching," was the only answer she offered, rubbing her eyes to discard the remnants of sleep still crusting her eyes half shut. "What are *you* doing here, other than tormenting me with your presence before I even have time to wake up?"

"Isn't that reason enough to be here at 8:00 a.m. on a Saturday, Cassidy?" he smirked, splaying his legs out and leaning back on his hands. She shot him a glare, which only made the dimples in the corner of his mouth deepen. "I'm figuring out some more choreo. Care to run through it with me?"

"No," she replied, rifling through the log-books on her desk for the one she would need to register the students.

"Oh, come on." Julian clucked his tongue and stood up, his approaching frame a tall shield against the blinding glow of the rising Sun. "I've figured out a lift we can try."

The thought of a lift sent dread rolling through her, but Nora feigned apathy as she inspected last week's register. "Didn't you hear the part about me biting off your head?"

"I'm terrified, really," he taunted, fingers clamping around her wrist as he pulled her away from the desk. "Come on. Just try this with me a minute."

"You're really going to make my life as hellish as possible for the next seven weeks, aren't you?" Her eyebrow twitched into an arch as he dragged her in front of the mirrors like she was nothing more than a heap of bones.

"Yep." Julian's eyes glinted as his hands found her hips. Even through her bundled layers of clothing, his touch was pressure enough that she flinched. If Julian noticed, he didn't comment, head bowed in the mirrors as he instructed her next movement in his ear. "We'll start with a simple one. I'm going to lift you by the waist, and I want you to reach up with one bent leg and both feet flexed. Just go with the movement."

Nora nodded, trying to ignore the nerves raging through her chest — trying not to think of the last time Julian had lifted her like this. It was a simple lift. Nothing could go wrong. Still, as his grip tightened, she shrank between his fingers.

"Ready?"

Another nod, this time weak as she swallowed down the anxiety. "Yeah."

"Go." He pushed her into the air with his unrelenting grasp. Her feet barely moved off the ground and her hands fell over Julian's own at her waist instead of reaching the way he'd told her to. She landed on stiff knees, body itching with the desire to get out of his grip and run. How could she do this? How could she let herself be lifted by him, dance with him in front of people?

"You need to reach," he repeated impatiently. "You barely moved."

"Sorry." Her words were hoarse and wavering.

Julian clenched his jaw, harsh wrinkles sinking into his forehead. "Let's try again."

His touch returned to her hips, causing her to wince involuntarily again.

"Stop doing that." The order was grave and too close to her ear, his chin brushing against her hair. "Stop shying away."

"Sorry," she repeated. "It's just that my whole body is repulsed by you. It's instinct."

He scoffed, low enough that it was more of a snarl. "I don't want to touch you anymore than you want to touch me, Cassidy. Do it right and we won't have to drag it out."

"Promise?" she breathed. His hands were bunching up her clothes now, desperate to get her in the air. She caved in defeat.

"Go."

She did, reaching for the ceiling as though there was something above her just out of reach. Julian's strength didn't falter, not even when her feet were well and truly off the ground with the rest of her. He lowered her gently despite the speed of the movement, and she landed with barely a noise.

"There we go," he praised, words only slightly tainted by arrogance. "Not so hard, was it?"

Nora scowled and peered over his shoulder. It was still early and nobody else had turned up yet, a fact that left her huffing with impatience. She was done with this, with him.

"Let's try another. I want you to go up the same, but this time, you're going to arch your back over my head."

"No," she blurted, heart dropping into her stomach. "That's too high."

"Oh, come on, Cassidy," he quipped. "We're already halfway there."

"I was still upright in the last one." She stepped away from him and shielded her body by hugging her torso. "No danger of us both falling and breaking our necks."

Julian narrowed his eyes quizzically. "You don't think I can lift you?"

"I think it's quite obvious that I can't be thrown about like other dancers."

"Why not?"

Nora could no longer look at him, she looked to the line of trophies gleaming on the shelves behind him instead. *Don't make me say it.* "You know why not."

"Nora," her name rushed out in an exasperated puff of breath, "I'm not a teenager anymore. Besides, that was a one-off mistake. I won't drop you again."

"I'm not a teenager anymore, either." She worried at her lip. "I'm heavier now and I'd like to stay on the ground, thank you."

The stifling silence that followed made her cringe. Her body was something she had made peace with but, standing here with the ghost of her teenage years haunting her every second and Julian's fingers itching to get a hold of her, she felt twice as large as she had before. She felt as though she was wearing a weighted suit she wanted to pull off and throw away, like she was taking up too much space. She always took up too much space, especially now, in the confines of the quiet she had induced.

"You're not heavy, Cassidy." His words were both delicate and forceful, sharp and soft, like getting hit with the blunt hilt of a sword rather than the steely point. "I can lift you, no problem. Trust me."

Her eyes scanned his face. She couldn't trust him; that was the problem. He was still the boy who had let her fall, the boy she hated, the boy who had joined in with the others in their teasing and name calling.

"Come here," he beckoned gently.

She obeyed as though in a trance, chin wobbling as she stood in front of him again. Her back burned with the weight of his gaze as his hands returned to her hips, this time not with any of the roughness he had shown a moment ago.

"Just try it for me. Please?"

Nora sucked in a trembling breath, catching his eyes in the mirror. There was no cocky smirk on his lips or wicked glint in his eyes now.

"If you drop me," she muttered, "I'm bringing you down with me."

A chuckle rumbled in his chest. "I won't let you go, Cassidy. Promise."

He lifted her with painstaking slowness, as though showing her that he was not afraid.

"I've got you," he reassured her as her toes curled, searching desperately for something to grasp onto. "Arch your back for me now."

She did, only because his hands were solid pillars beneath her, unwavering. Her spine pulled with the strain — she hadn't had the chance to warm up yet — but she draped herself in an arc above his head anyway, letting her hands dangle down toward his spine. For a moment, she felt as stable and tall as architecture. She felt weightless.

"See?" She could hear the grin in Julian's voice as he lowered her carefully. "I've got you."

A soft, mangled noise of relief escaped her as her feet grounded themselves on the wood again. Julian's touch lingered as she caught his smile in the mirror.

"Well." The new voice was shocking enough to drive Nora away from Julian in a heartbeat. Constance stood by the door, a thin smile gracing her lips as she eyed them both. "Things seem to be going well here. Watch your arms, Nora. You never straighten them properly."

Nora fought the urge to roll her eyes. Constance had not once complimented her without tagging criticism onto it, too. "We were just practicing."

"So I see," she nodded, flicking on the studio's ceiling lights. Her weathered face was a ghastly yellow beneath the fluorescents, no other color lived on her cheeks or in her eyes. Even her hair seemed whiter now.

"Are you feeling okay, Constance?" Nora couldn't help but ask, though she knew it was sure to get her a lecture. "You don't look very well."

"I could say the same of you." Constance pursed her lips as she wandered across the floor. "Is this how you wish to present yourself to your students?"

The jab might have done less harm if she wasn't still standing beside Julian. As it were, she tucked her flyaway hair behind her ear and shuffled uncomfortably.

"If you need my assistance, I'll be in my office."

"Okay." Nora freed herself of her thick scarf, glad when Constance disappeared into the dark corridor without another word.

"She's always such a charming old lady, isn't she?" Julian added, slipping on his socks as the first of her students arrived.

Nora flashed him a tight smile as she gathered her logbook. "Almost as charming as you."

Julian put a hand to his chest, feigning hurt. "And here I thought we were getting along for a minute, Cassidy."

Nora scoffed. "When pigs fly, perhaps."

She left him sitting by the mirrors, trying to forget the way his hands had curled around her hips so tightly... and how that touch had seemed to switch from heavy and uncomfortable to completely soothing and steadfast in an instant.

Perhaps they *had* been getting along, just for a moment.

And perhaps Nora had enjoyed it, just for a moment.

Seven

Julian couldn't suppress the groan that escaped him as he pulled himself up from the floor of his father's garage. He was sore after the first week of rehearsing almost every night with Nora. She had been pushing him harder than he liked to admit with the choreography, with new moves and positions he hadn't tried before, and it was taking its toll now. Working here on his feet all day wasn't helping, either.

"Can you stop grumbling?" Graham, his father, nagged as he popped open the hood of the car next to him. It was only midday, yet the lines in his aging face were filled with black grease, as though he had just walked out of a burning building. "You sound like one of the cars."

"Sorry," Julian muttered, wiping his face with a dirtied rag and then cramming it back into the pocket of his overalls.

"What's wrong with you anyway? Dancing again?" The way he said "dancing" with such disdain did not go unnoticed.

Julian rolled his eyes at the question. He had been dancing non-stop since the age of six; there was no "again" about it, no matter how much of his father loved to pretend otherwise. "I'm working on my audition for Phoenix. That reminds me… if I get in, I won't be able to work here anymore. You might have to hire somebody else willing to slave away for you."

Graham lifted his head to look at Julian. His dark eyes held a dangerous glint in them, one that Julian had learned not to shy away from anymore, though he still felt the instinct rise up in his stomach. "What the hell is 'Phoenix'?"

"An international dance company." It wasn't the first time Julian had mentioned it, but he knew better than to point out his father's ignorance. "I'd be traveling for a big part of the year and based in London during rehearsals."

Graham shook his head, a sneer curling on his lips as he returned to the deteriorated engine in front of him. "That brother of yours better have his head screwed on before I lose faith in both my offspring. I told your mother she should never have taken you to those fucking dance lessons."

"Lucky Mom doesn't listen to a word you say," he retorted, nostrils flaring as he twizzled his wrench in his hands. He hated this place. He hated the gray walls and the stink of gasoline. He hated working on cars when he could have — should have — been dancing. He hated his father, who would always see him and his brother as something lesser because they didn't choose to be covered head to toe in oil all day every day like him.

The sooner Julian got out of here, the better.

He was glad when a car rolled up outside and ran out to greet the new customer before Graham had even the chance to notice it. It was an old, sad little hatchback that coughed out a rattle as it braked. Julian knew without having to look that he would have to change the brake rotors, at the very least.

The last person he had been expecting to climb out of the driver's side was Nora Cassidy, yet she did, swinging her hair over one shoulder as she slammed the door shut. The hinges creaked against the force.

"You missed the turn for the scrap yard about a half mile back that way." He pointed down the winding road, lined by a sorry sight of dull trees shedding their amber leaves.

"Ha ha," Nora replied without a hint of amusement.

"Has dearest grandmother not been keeping up with your trust fund?"

She scowled, twirling her key chain around her finger and leaning against the car. "You know, there's another mechanic on the other side of town. I'd be happy to take my business elsewhere."

Julian opened his mouth, about to express how absolutely fine he would be with that, when his father interrupted behind him.

"Excuse my son. He has the manners of a pig."

Julian was half tempted to snort and point out that those manners had been inherited from

Graham himself, but instead, he rolled his eyes as Graham emerged from the garage's shadows and moved to stand beside him. He wiped his coarse fingers across his overalls — about as much cleanliness he ever showed and always for the sole sake of customers.

"Dad, this is my dance partner, Nora Cassidy," he introduced. "Her grandmother owns the studio."

Graham's polite façade fell from his face in an instant, his cruel lips twitching downward as he scoured Nora's appearance from head to toe. To Nora's credit, she didn't falter, only crossed her arms over her chest impatiently.

"What happened to that other girlfriend of yours?"

Julian's hands crumpled into fists, but he kept his features smooth, expressionless, unwilling to feed his father's constant need to tear him and everything linked to his dance career down. "Sienna moved to Edinburgh last week. We're not together anymore."

"Will you be coming to the showcase, Mr. Walker?" Nora questioned in a voice that was far too sickly sweet to be genuine.

Graham blinked. Even his eyelashes were caked in dirt. "No. And my name's not Walker." He pointed up at the sign above the door reading *Hart's Auto Repair* as he headed back into the garage. "That's his mother's."

Nora's attention turned back to Julian. "I see

where you get your wonderful manners from."

Julian pursed his lips and dragged her away from the car, out of his father's earshot. "Just don't say a word about Fraser taking lessons to him. He doesn't know."

Concern softened Nora's features for a moment. "Why not?"

"He doesn't approve." Bitterness laced the words as he shot a glare in the direction of the garage. "Wants us to be just like him."

"Oh." She worried at her lip and looked adorable doing it. Clearly, Nora had never had trouble with her family not approving of her dance classes. White hot jealousy snaked in Julian's stomach, but he pushed it down as he leaned a hand against the roof of her car. He didn't want her sympathy, didn't like the way it swam in her grass-green eyes, so he continued before she could offer it.

"What's up with the car anyway, Cassidy? Besides everything?"

She cast him a dithering look. "It's making a noise when I brake."

"What kind of noise?"

"A...." she trailed off, looking at the car as though it was a dying patient on a hospital bed and not just a piece of junk. "I don't know, a strangled cat noise."

Julian clamped his lips together to keep from laughing. "So like you when you sing?"

"You haven't heard me sing," Nora glared,

though patches of color seeped into her cheeks.

"Unfortunately, I have. You sing under your breath all the bloody time." It was true: He had noticed it the other day, when they were warming up before practice. That was only the tip of the iceberg of annoying Nora Cassidy habits, too: She played with her hair too often, pulled on her socks inside out, and tripped over his foot in the middle of the routine, as though she had forgotten she was performing a duet, not to mention the long nails that carved scratches into his arms every time he went near her, like she was, in fact, some sort of stray cat.

"I'm here to get my car fixed, not be critiqued on my singing," she shot back, keys rattling as she put her hands on her hips — another annoying Nora Cassidy quirk.

"Alright." Julian patted the roof of the car, surprised when it didn't cause the whole vehicle to fall apart, and then examined the rest of it. The paint job was battered by grazes and rust: a hopeless case if Julian had ever seen one. "Have you checked for strangled cats?"

"Do you treat all of your customers like this?"

Julian bared his teeth in a wide grin. "Only my favorites."

"Maybe I'll complain to your manager." She cast her eyes over to Graham in warning. Another streak of irritation shot through him.

"How long has it been making the noise?"

"I don't know." She shrugged in deliberation. The movement wafted the scent of her fruity perfume toward him and caused his nose to itch, but he didn't dare touch his face when his hands were this grimy. "A couple of weeks, I think."

A huff of disbelief hitched in his throat. "And you waited until now to get it checked?"

"Well, I was hoping it might just... I don't know, sort itself out."

"Oh, yeah, I get that. You never know when the magical pixies living under your hood might do you a solid and fix your car, save you a trip to the mechanic." Julian shook his head and rounded the car to examine it from the front. "You're an idiot, Cassidy. You're lucky it didn't end badly."

"I don't know," Nora shot back. "Coming here and having to talk to you isn't my definition of luck. I think I'd prefer a crash, to be honest."

Julian found that the anger in his chest was roiling now — not at her snappy retorts, because he was used to those, but at the fact that she hadn't had it checked sooner. If it *were* the braking rotors that had gone, it would have only taken one bad move on the road to cause an accident, and with the weather getting icier....

He pushed the concern down, stored it away where it couldn't reach him, and told himself he was only upset because it would have ruined the Winter Showcase rather than the absurd fact that he might actually care.

"You want to leave? Feel free. Go get yourself into an accident, and then see how cocky you are."

"But then you'd have to find somebody who actually *wants* to dance with you." She didn't miss a beat before replying. It was a duet in itself, all this back and forth. Dancing around, trying to make each other squirm. Julian couldn't even remember when it had begun, though he was certain it was well before the infamous incident at her last dance competition. Before that, though, it had been friendly banter, at most. Sometimes, now, it got far more vicious. Most of the time, he still enjoyed it. Hating Nora Cassidy was a hobby that came straight after dancing on his list of preferred activities.

"That'd be no fun at all." His nose wrinkled mockingly. Then he remembered the leaflet he had shoved in the pocket of his jeans this morning and patted down his overalls to search for it. "That reminds me."

Nora's eyes gleamed with amusement as he wriggled his hands down to fish out the pamphlet from his back pocket. "Is this a new dance move?"

Julian ignored her and shoved it into her hands. She left it dangling out in front of her in disgust.

"Do I want to know where this has been?"

He clucked his tongue. Did she ever stop with the wise cracks? "It's a leaflet for a Phoenix show. The contemporary troupe are performing not too far from here this week, so I bought us tickets for Friday afternoon."

"Oh, good, I didn't have anything better to do." Though she pretended it was a hindrance, Julian noticed the interest gleaming beneath the surface of her eyes as she scanned it once over.

"You don't, actually," he responded smugly. "Checked your schedule."

"Yes, the schedule that is my life." She handed the pamphlet back with an arched eyebrow. "I have no friends, no social life, no hobbies. Only dance and you. The things recorded on that piece of paper."

"I assumed as much."

"I'm not paying you to stand about jabbering, Julian," Graham called, his voice echoing around the garage and putting an end to their conversation.

"I'll leave you to it." Nora shuffled, as though reluctant to leave the car. "Look, this was my father's car. Take care of it, please."

That explained the condition of it. Her father had died when Julian was only ten or eleven. It wasn't something that Nora mentioned often, though he remembered the stifling silence that had settled like fog across the dance studio in the weeks that followed his passing, not just in her but everyone. Her father had been a constant and uplifting presence in the face of Constance's strict rule, and everybody had felt the loss.

"It's in safe hands, Cassidy." He displayed his blackened hands, fingers dancing across the air.

"Promise. I'll have it ready for you by the end of the week."

She hesitated before nodding, running her hands across the marred metal before stepping away from it. "Then I'll see you tonight. Thanks."

His heart almost broke at the solemn, lingering glance she cast over her shoulder before she began her walk down the dirt road.

Eight

The address on the back of the pamphlet hadn't brought Julian anywhere close to the area he'd been expecting. There wasn't a theater in sight, only a museum shaped like an egg contained within a shell of glass. He shut off the engine and pulled it out again for another look, but the address was the same one displayed on the Maps app on his phone. Nora had graciously held it the entire ride here while giving him the wrong direction at every roundabout they encountered — a talent, considering the directions were written in front of her, clear as day.

It had been a long, painful ride spent trying not to lose his head, and it showed now on both of their faces. He could feel that his features were taut as he pulled the keys out of the ignition and leaned back in his seat. Beside him, she locked his phone and threw it onto his lap without looking at him.

"We made it in one piece," he offered, running his hands over his stubbly chin. He hadn't shaved this morning, since they weren't dancing and he wasn't working. Not that he couldn't dance with facial hair, but Nora had complained about it in the second rehearsal when it brushed her shoulder during the sequence, and he'd caved when it was brought up another three times after — in exchange for her cutting and filing down her nails.

"Don't speak so soon." Her mutter was monotone as she glared out at the museum. "We still have the ride back."

Julian grimaced at the thought, but a retort didn't come. He was too nervous. Anxiety roiled in his gut like a tempest, reminding him of how badly he wanted this with every crashing wave. What he might see today could either make or break him, inspire him or show him he wasn't good enough to be part of the company at all.

"Any idea why they're not performing at a theater?" Nora questioned finally, freeing herself of her seat belt and untucking her hair from her scarf so it splayed in bronze waves across her shoulders. She had made more of an effort with her appearance today, her lips a glossy peach and cheeks stained pink, although Julian couldn't tell whether it was from the cold or makeup. Either way, he had fought the urge to tell her she looked nice when he'd picked her up from her apartment this morning and glimpsed the floral dress hiding beneath her coat.

He had been expecting her to live in a fancy complex at the edge of town considering her grandmother's wealth, but her red brick building was just like any other. Just like his, and not that far away, either. She kept surprising him.

"Let me consult my crystal ball."

"God, you're touchy today," she huffed under her breath.

"I'm not touchy," he argued, though he could hear the impatience fringing his words just as clearly. He couldn't help it. Couldn't help the way his leg jiggled as he waited for the clock on his dashboard to signal an appropriate time to go in, since they were unfashionably early and the parking lot was still dead. "You're just annoying me."

"Well, you annoy me all the time, so I guess we're even." She shot him a bitter sideways glance. "Are you nervous?"

"No." His lie was poorly executed, a sharp, abrupt syllable that made him sound as though she was accusing him of something — something he was guilty of. To distract himself, he pulled down the mirror and smoothed down the sides of his hair.

"You are," she insisted, voice high in disbelief. In such a confined space, it pierced his eardrums and made him wince. "Why?"

"I'm not nervous," he ground out, eyes narrowing. There was movement at the front doors as a man wearing a suit took up his position and a crowd he hadn't noticed before began to head in. Julian sighed in relief and slapped the mirror back up.

The unease humming through his veins sparked into untamed electricity as he murmured, "Showtime."

∞ ∞ ∞

The performance was otherworldly. The company's stage was a three-story museum, and they led the audience up staircases and across balconies as the afternoon light played across their stark white costumes. Nora tried not to acknowledge the fact that every single one of them was shaped like Julian — lean, muscular, athletic — and none of them burst from their Lycra the way that Nora's body would have. The way that it had.

Of course, she was used to seeing slim dancers everywhere she went, but she was still — naively, perhaps — waiting for the day when she would not be the only plus-size dancer she knew.

Regardless, the dance took her breath away. They followed the dancers through sections lit by old, guttering bulbs and past mirrors, where they performed duets with their reflections. The solos had enraptured her with the anticipation of never knowing how they would move next, the groups, the unison, and the echoes even more so. It was clever. It was beautiful. It meant something that could not be reduced to the English language, as all the best dances couldn't.

It worried her.

Not because Julian was not good enough to be a part of the group — she had pictured him perfectly flitting around with the rest of them — but because the two of them had only choreographed the first fifty seconds, and it was a flat, basic sequence in comparison. They would have to be better.

As soon as the applause broke, Julian tugged Nora through the crowd by her elbow. He stopped only when a plump, dark-haired woman intercepted his path with a warm smile. Julian's face flickered with recognition, but Nora did not find her at all familiar.

"Julian Walker." Her lips spread thinly into a pleased smile as she held out her hand. "I was hoping to see you at one of our shows. Getting a taste of what might be to come?"

Julian let go of Nora to shake the woman's hand firmly. When he pulled away, Nora glimpsed the trembling of his fingers. "Miss Phoenix," he greeted tautly. "It's lovely to see you again. The performance was absolutely spectacular."

Only then did it dawn on Nora who she was: Jennifer Phoenix, the director and founder of the dance company they had just watched perform... and the woman who would decide Julian's future. Nora couldn't help but scrutinise her, her heart hammering wildly in her chest. She was dressed in a pinstriped suit, but other than that, she held no air of superiority about her. Not like Constance. She could have been any other member of the audience.

And though Nora tried not to notice, Jennifer's body was curvy and far from slender. Just like

Nora's. It caused something in her to lift. Jennifer was a director of an internationally renowned dance company, probably had been a dancer herself or perhaps still was, and she was like Nora. Not muscular, slim, or stuck-up.

"Oh, Julian." Jennifer waved a dismissive hand modestly. "I'd say flattery will get you nowhere, but it just wouldn't be true." Her gaze fell on Nora, warm eyes drinking her in slowly. "And who did you bring today?"

Julian glanced at Nora as though forgetting she was standing there. Nora forced herself not to shrivel beneath the weight of their sudden attention.

"This is—"

"Nora Cassidy," Nora finished for Julian, shaking Jennifer's hand gingerly. "I'll be performing with Julian at the Winter Showcase."

She waited for the disbelief or the sneering, but it never came. Instead, Jennifer only arched one perfectly shaped eyebrow, her smile deepening as though the information pleased her. "You're Julian's dance partner?"

"For now," Nora nodded.

"And do you hope to become a dancer on a more professional level, too? We are still holding open auditions next week, and I'd be quite happy to rearrange a few things to fit you in."

"O-oh," Nora stammered, stunned. "Thank you, but I'm actually more of a teacher than a dancer. I'm only doing this as a favor."

"She's modest," Julian interjected, patting Nora on the shoulder as though they were old pals rather than practically enemies. "She's a great dancer."

"Well, if you change your mind, give us a call." Nora nearly slumped with relief when Jennifer's attention turned back to Julian. "And as for you, I'll be seeing you in two weeks for your callback. Best of luck."

"Thank you," Julian ground out politely, and then, under his breath as Jennifer left, "I'll need it."

Nora could sense the stress and doubt radiating from Julian as they spilled out of the museum, the bitter November air a bleak tug back into the real world after the last few hours spent watching magic. Nora didn't dare ask what he thought of the show or Jennifer's offer as they ambled back to the car in silence. He unlocked the door with an unnecessarily aggressive jolt of his wrist and, after they had both climbed in, slammed it just as roughly.

The air was thick with words neither of them dared say. Julian didn't start the car, and Nora didn't make a move to fix her seat belt. Instead, they just stared out, Julian's knuckles white where they clenched the steering wheel. He looked as though he was contemplating whether to fling his head or his fists into the thing.

"She was nice," Nora observed finally.

"We're not good enough." A cold, sharp retaliation.

Nora chewed on her bottom lip, resting her head against the window. "No, we just need to be better, and we will be."

Julian's sneer cleaved his face in two. Gone was the amicable, kind man who had sung Nora's praises a moment ago. "Inspirational, Cassidy. Does your grandmother pay you for your wisdom as well as your teaching?"

"Oh, stop it," she snapped. "Phoenix clearly likes you. We'll work it out. We'll get some props, maybe try to find another song."

"Props and a new song won't fix all our problems." The words were a hoarse vibration in his chest, throat bobbing as he swallowed.

Nora sighed. "Fine," she decided, clicking on her seat belt with newfound determination. "Then give it up."

He faltered, turning to her finally. His brown eyes swam with emotions she had never imagined him to possess before: panic, despair, self-doubt. It was enough to make her resolve sag with her shoulders. This mattered to him. It *really* mattered. Nora hadn't realized quite how much before, though it made sense, if he was desperate enough to ask for her help in the first place. It left her wishing she *could* help now. That was her problem: She always wanted to help, even if it was to benefit someone she hated.

"What?" he breathed, his face full of shadows.

"Give it up," she repeated, feigning nonchalance as she gazed out of the window. The carpark was nearly empty again, withering trees separating them from the road they would be back on at any moment. "If you honestly think you're not good enough — *we're* not good enough — and there's no way to change that, give it up. Why bother?"

"You don't mean that." Still, his features hardened with determination. Julian Walker was not the type of man who would sit by and be told to give up, and Nora had known that, known that the mere suggestion would stoke the searing fire in him. "What is this, reverse psychology?"

Nora shrugged. "Did it work?"

"No."

"Good. Saves me another six weeks of headaches and late nights with you."

Julian shook his head, the corner of his mouth twitching as he put his key in the ignition and turned. The engine broke the thick tension with its purr, reminding Nora that there was a world outside of this car — a world they needed to return to. "You're not that lucky, Cassidy."

"I can hope." And then, because she had not chased the shadows on his face away completely, and because she had forgotten that Julian Walker loved to tease her every word, and because he had said something nice about her in front of Jennifer Phoenix, she muttered, "You know, you're as good as every one of those dancers in there. You've practiced your whole life to get here. It'll pay off."

"Not getting into this company isn't a choice, Nora." To her surprise, there was no mocking there. "I need this to work."

The honesty sucked the breath out of Nora. Rain began to patter on the windowpane, dark clouds rolling in above as the Sun began to sink behind the pines. She tucked her hair behind her ear and buried herself further into her seat.

Without daring to look at him, she said, "Then we'll make it work."

Nine

When Nora had asked Julian to drop her off at the café, she hadn't expected him to get out of the car and follow her in. It was late, dark, and cold, and she had to dodge the puddles as she stepped in. They were greeted by the bell above the door. Annie was in the middle of closing up, half of the chairs already placed on the old, round tables and the white mugs lined up in their entirety on top of the coffee machine.

At their entrance, her friend lifted her attention from the counter she was wiping down, eyes crinkling with happiness, as though she had not seen Nora just a few days ago when she had done a quick lunchtime shift.

"I've been waiting for you!" Giddiness bubbled from her as she rounded the counter but simmered slightly when she noticed Julian towering behind Nora. "Oh, you brought... him."

"I can leave—" Julian began but was cut off by Annie's high-pitched scream.

"I'm getting married!" She displayed the silver band on her finger, hands so close that Nora went cross-eyed in her attempt to look at it. "Meg, get in here!"

Nora couldn't stifle the squeal that fell from her mouth as she gripped Annie's hand to get a better look. It was a simple ring — better that way, because Annie always had her hands in the sink or a ball of bread dough for the café's famous cinnamon rolls — but it suited her delicate fingers well, even with the chipped nails. "Oh, my goodness!"

Meg appeared from the beaded curtain behind the counter a moment later, her expression split by a smile so wide it hurt Nora to see. "You said we'd tell her together!"

"I couldn't wait," Annie protested as Nora skipped to Meg and gathered her in a tight hug.

"Congratulations, Meg! Who asked who?"

"I did," Meg replied. "Or I started to, and then Annie started a proposal of her own. Turns out we both had the same plans." It wasn't until they weaved back through the piled chairs that she stopped and frowned. "Who's this?"

"I'm Julian Walker." Julian flashed an uncomfortable wave. "I was, er, just here to drop Nora off. Sorry for intruding."

"Oh, no, don't be silly." Meg seemed not to notice Annie's daggers as she inspected Julian's tall frame. "Any friend of Nora's is a friend of ours."

"We're not friends," Nora and Julian countered with a more precise unison than they had yet to achieve in the dance studio.

"I should go, actually." Julian shuffled uncomfortably on his feet. He hadn't said much on the ride home, other than when his road rage had slipped through and he'd muttered a string of angry curse words to the driver who'd cut in front of him. Still, his almond eyes flickered to Nora now, and any residual anger or fear no longer flickered there. "See you tomorrow morning?"

Nora hummed her agreement, already inspecting the ring on Meg's finger. This one was embedded with silver stones that cast slivers of light onto her brown skin where the fluorescents hit it, since Meg was bound to pose less of a hazard in taking care of it. "Bright and early."

"Congratulations again," Julian said before leaving.

Annie scoffed immediately, sinking down onto one of the few chairs that hadn't been put away yet. "You're an amateur, Meg."

"What?" Meg frowned, glancing from Nora to Annie. "I thought he was nice."

"Julian Walker is *not* nice. He made Nora's life hell growing up. We do not like him."

"Alright, let's not talk about Julian now." Nora slid behind the counter and rifled through the fridge. A bottle of champagne that had been stored there for New Year's Eve was hidden at the back, she pulled it out eagerly. "You're getting married! Let's celebrate."

"Well, we've already decided on a date." Even with Nora's back turned, she could hear the grin in Meg's voice.

Ceramic clinked as Annie pulled three mugs down from the coffee machine. It was pumpkin spice latte and hot chocolate season, so the glasses they usually kept out for iced tea had been tucked away in a cupboard somewhere for warmer days.

"You don't waste any time."

"Why wait?" Love softened Meg's dark eyes to honey as she cast Annie a look that belonged only to her. It was enough to make Nora's stomach wrench with unwelcome sadness, though of course, she was ecstatic for them both. She just couldn't imagine anybody loving her the way they loved each other, and it made her… not jealous but reflective and perhaps a little bit dejected. She wanted it someday. It had been a long time since she had last felt loved. "We booked The Willow for the first Saturday of December."

Nora's eyes widened. "December of this year? As in, a few weeks away?"

"Yep," Annie chimed in as she poured the champagne with the steady hands of an experienced barista. "It's going to be just the two of us at the registry office, and then we'll celebrate with our small circle of friends and family later on. That way, we can spend our first Christmas together as wives."

"Sounds perfect. Cheers to that." They clinked mugs before Nora gulped down the champagne, the bubbles pricking at her throat and the sweetness making her mouth water. "I suppose I'd better look for a dress."

Ten

To his surprise, Julian was not the first in the dance studio the next day. Though their practices at 8:00 a.m. on a Saturday — now, apparently, turned 7:30 a.m. — hadn't been on the schedule, after their first week, it had become just as regular a rehearsal as any other.

Nora was halfway to the ceiling on a pair of ladders, stringing a long, silk curtain up with the rigs usually used for lighting. It was a flimsy, dusty fabric that cobwebs clung to. Julian recognized it from one of their earlier group dances, when they had danced behind it as nothing more than silhouettes to gradually get used to being exposed to an audience.

"What's this?" he questioned as he shut out the cold.

Nora jumped on the ladders and put a hand to her chest. "Jesus."

"Careful, Cassidy," he warned, only half teasing as he hung up his coat and kicked off his shoes. "Breaking your ankle on me now won't get you out of this."

He had not realized how tactless the joke was until it was out of his mouth and her face had darkened. She had broken her ankle at that competition. Her last competition. Because of him. Because he had been an arrogant idiot who had let her fall.

"This is a curtain, Julian," was all she said, tongue poking out as she fixed the final hook. "People usually use them to cover their windows."

Julian rolled his eyes and positioned himself at the bottom of the ladder. It was rocking a little too much for his liking as she stretched to the ceiling, so he weighted it down with his foot and hands. "I mean why is it here, clever clogs?"

"Well, as you so kindly announced yesterday, our dance isn't good enough yet." She began her descent on steady feet, hopping off the last step with an energy he hadn't seen from her before. "And while props might not solve all our problems, they can't hurt. So I got up early to search the basement this morning and found this old thing."

"You did this?" Julian raised an eyebrow, grazing his fingers over the silk curtain in surprise.

"No need to thank me," she replied, slapping her hands together as though she'd just finished a hard day of labor. "I only did it so you'd stop bellyaching."

"Good. For a second there, I thought you might actually be being nice."

"Nice to you?" Nora grimaced. "Gross."

Julian didn't bother to hide his smirk as he shook his head and stretched his arms over his chest to warm up. "You're not very good at pretending, Cassidy."

"Who's pretending?" Nora glanced up at the curtain, twirling it on her fingers. He could practically see the ideas ticking in her head. Nora was a lot of things, and a good choreographer had always been one of them. He had no doubt that she'd think up something good today, even if he wasn't so keen to admit it. "I just think we need to do more than just dance, y'know? This might inspire us."

Julian ignored the flutter in his stomach at the word "us." As though they were in this together now. As though they could get through it so long as they were. He had never felt that before, not with Sienna or anyone that had come before her. And Sienna certainly wouldn't have come here at the crack of dawn to hang up a curtain and figure out new ideas.

Nora Cassidy was doing more than just granting him a few favors at this point. She was practically a lifesaver. He hated that fact more than anything else that had happened between them, because it meant that he owed her.

The last thing Julian wanted was to be indebted to somebody who hated his guts.

∞∞∞

Half an hour later, they had already come up with something a thousand times more creative than anything else they'd done. Their first sequence was all light and shadow play, with their silhouettes weaving in and out of each other, in and out of the curtains, separating them and then pulling them back together again. Pride swelled in Nora as they mapped out their next few movements. They involved a lift that landed with Julian on the floor and Nora wrapped around him on top.

Just for a moment, she could feel his heavy breath on her face, smell the spice of his cologne, and feel his shirt crumpling beneath her fingers. She paused, losing herself in the overwhelming suddenness of it all. He licked his lips and gazed up at her as though he felt it, too.

"Sorry," she said, realizing she had been pinning him down with the weight of her body. Her cheeks flushed scarlet as she made to climb off him, but his hands gripped her waist and kept her there. His touch sent a burst of warmth low in her belly.

"You're okay," Julian breathed softly. He'd shaved this morning, his brown skin silken around his jaw and chin — for her. Because she had complained about the rough stubble in moments like these, when they were so close that she was breathing him in.

"Where do we go from here?" Nora shifted with the desperation to rid him of her weight, though it didn't seem to bother him.

His hands slid up until they were wrapped around the soft flesh protecting her rib cage. Her skin splintered from the unexpected touch, she

RACHEL BOWDLER

tried to hide the way it made her shiver. "You think we can fit in another lift?"

"No," she replied bluntly. "What about a leg extension?"

She demonstrated, bracketing his hips with her knees and rolling onto the front one to sweep her leg out behind her. Her arms painted an arc in the air, and the momentum allowed her to roll off Julian without having to face anymore discomfort.

"Alright," he agreed, rolling onto his knees. "That gives us a chance for some unison at the front here. Maybe we can take a little bit of the sequence we already had and slot it in. Let's go from the top of the old one, shall we?"

They did, dancing to a silent harmony as they brushed across the floor with movements their muscles had vowed to remember. Nora didn't notice her grandmother watching them until they stopped, and she nearly jumped out of her skin for a second time that morning.

"Is this a dance meant for a funeral?" Constance questioned by way of greeting, folding her coat over her arm. Though she was tiny and hunched, her presence took up enough of the dance studio that the air turned cold. "There's no emotion there. The two of you aren't connecting."

Nora was glad when Julian spoke so she wouldn't have to. "We're working on it, Miss Cassidy."

"Work harder," she demanded. "You need to build a partnership here. Perhaps try having a conversation that is not about dance every now and again."

The suggestion shocked them both into silence. Constance Cassidy implying that they shouldn't focus wholly on dance? That their lives must include something other than this studio? Were these the first signs of senility?

Nora didn't have a chance to find out. Constance, as always, tread across the floor and straight into her office as though she could no longer stand the sight of either of them.

"Does that woman ever have anything positive to say?" Julian pondered with a sharp release of breath.

"Oh, Julian. You've been here since you were a kid. Don't you know better by now?" Nora shook her head hopelessly and picked up her water bottle from the side of the floor, checking the clock. It wouldn't be long until her students arrived.

As though sensing it, Julian cleared his throat. "Have you got a minute to spare before classes start?"

Nora frowned in suspicion as she swigged her water. "I suppose. Why?"

"Put your coat on, Cassidy." Julian jerked his head toward the door. "You'll see."

Nora huffed as she obeyed and followed him outside. The cold was unrelenting, the promise of winter's first snowfall palpable enough that Nora could taste the crisp freshness of it. The only thing that served as respite was her father's car parked on the front of the lot, right next to her grand-mother's.

Her father's.

Even after all these years, she still saw it as his and not hers — a loan, as though he would one day come back for it. The realization sent a pang of grief through her, as sharp as the day she lost him, when she was not quite a teenager but not quite a child.

"It's ready?" was all she could croak out.

"Yep," Julian grinned. "Gave it a test run on the way here. Even ironed out some of its kinks."

"What?" Nora stumbled closer to inspect the car. Some of the paint scratches had been buffered out, and it was altogether shinier and sturdier. A brand-new freshener hung on the mirror in the window, and she could tell the wind-shield had been replaced, for it no longer had its old cracks. "What did you do to it? I can't afford all this."

"It's taken care of," he reassured her, scrap-ing his hand across the roof smugly. "Consider it recompense for all of the effort you're putting into being a pain in my ass."

Tears gathered in her eyes as she looked up in awe. "I truly can't stand you." Her words, for once, were not thick with hate but with appreci-ation. She had been worried when her brakes went, she would have to give the car up, along with every other part of her father she had lost. Now, it had life in it yet. Julian must have spent hours on the old heap of ruined metal. Hours he didn't really have.

"I know," Julian replied, understanding smoothing his features into a smile that was not cocky or bitter but kind. "My heart bleeds every day because of it. Promise."

Nora let just a glimmer of her own smile seep through her uncommitted scowl. Julian only chuckled and threw her the keys.

"I hope you know this means you're giving me a ride home tonight, Cassidy."

"Absolutely not." Her words were light as she cradled the familiar weight in her hand before pocketing it. "I hope you like the bus."

Eleven

Nora had been waiting for snow all weekend with jittery anticipation. As soon as the first flake fell on Monday afternoon, she braved the creepy crawlies to dig out the old Christmas decorations from the basement and hauled them into the studio, dust and cobwebs trailing behind her. She thanked the heavens that Constance wasn't here today to witness the mess.

Nobody was, save for Julian, of course. The light dusting had turned quickly into a blizzard, and her students had canceled not long after because of the roads. They had rehearsed for a few hours before Julian decided to work on his call back piece, leaving Nora to string the holiday lights and set up the Christmas tree. Every so often, he'd interrupt to ask her opinion on something or she'd choreograph a small section, but other than that, it was eerily quiet. Quiet enough that she could hear the pipes dripping with ice water outside and imagined the faint fluttering of the flakes against the windows.

Nora let out a sigh of content as she fixed the baubles on the branches. She loved snow and Christmas, even if it caused chaos and she hated how cold it could get. In here, though, that didn't matter. She was safe, with Julian's piano piece and padding feet her only backdrop.

Almost perfect. *Almost*.

It would have been if he didn't talk so much.

When she'd just about finished, save for plugging in the lights, she checked the clock and realized it was later than she'd thought — going on nine. Julian was in his own world as he figured out his choreography with slow, lazy steps, expression tightened into hard lines that showed his concentration.

"Are you planning on leaving tonight?" she asked finally. She wanted to turn the fluorescents off and see how the studio looked lit by only the Christmas lights, and she didn't think Julian would appreciate dancing in the darkness or putting up with her excitement when she saw how beautiful it was.

"Sorry." For once, he had no retort, too lost in his own head to even try. *Good*, Nora thought. She was exhausted and didn't have it in her to offer witty remarks tonight. She had gotten used to having him around, no longer so irked by just the mere presence of him, but she would still rather him go home now. "I'm more than capable of locking up if you want to go home."

"I don't," she sighed. "I want to admire my work."

Julian finally broke his focus enough to smirk. He gestured at nothing in particular.

"Please, be my guest."

Though it wasn't ideal, Nora couldn't stand to wait another moment, so she plugged everything in and turned out the overhead lights. It was beautiful. For a moment, she wasn't in the studio at all but somewhere warm and comforting and golden. With the main lights off, she could make out the snow falling in thick chunks outside. It was still wild, the incessant white dust blowing in with a whistling wind — too wild to contemplate moving yet.

In fact....

The snow had piled at the doors, reaching the same height as Nora's waist. Dread rippled in her stomach as she tried to open the door and found it completely iced over. "Julian."

"What?" A light irritation seeped into his tone, but then he looked up and saw what Nora was trying to do — and why. He swore under his breath and pushed Nora's hand away so he could try the handle himself. Even with his strength, it barely moved — and even if it did, how could they drive in this? The snow was falling so hard Nora could glimpse only the orange glow of the streetlights in the distance. Past that, she would not be able to see her own hand if she was out in it.

"Fancy crawling out of Constance's window?"

Nora shook her head in irritation. "And then what? We can't go anywhere in this."

Julian squinted as he surveyed the night

again, a muscle twitching his jaw. "Then it's going to be a long, long night, Cassidy."

"Maybe it'll stop in an hour or so." Even as she said it, she knew there was no hope. When it snowed like this here, it didn't give up so easily. Still, she wasn't about to just resign herself to a night trapped in the studio with Julian Walker, of all people.

"Well, Constance did say we needed to bond." Humor danced on his lips, as though he was finding entertainment in all of this. "Maybe she paid the weatherman."

"This is your fault. Did you not read the weather forecast this morning?"

"Did *you*?" he retorted sharply.

The answer, of course, was no, but she didn't bother to say so. Instead, she wrapped her arms around herself. It wasn't all that cold yet, but it would be if they had to stay, and she felt a phantom draught reach her just thinking about it. "I'm going to search for some blankets in case we're here a while."

"Wishful thinking?"

Again, no answer. If she was going to be here for a while, Nora would have to preserve her energy for more important things — like being trapped in the studio all night with a man she despised.

Twelve

"Any change?" Blisters were beginning to form on the bottom of Julian's toes from all the pirouetting. They hadn't put the lights back on. It was comforting to dance with only his mirrored silhouette guiding him, the tree lights blurring as he spun and leaped.

Nora stood by the door, a tartan scarf draped over her shoulders. It was the best she had been able to find in lost and found, save for a few hoodies. Her face was reflected in the pane of glass, solemn and dappled by the snow lashing down outside. He didn't need her to reply to know that it was still bad.

"No." She let loose an exhausted breath and broke her stare to look at him. "What are we going to do?"

Julian shrugged and pulled on his sweater and socks, both sticking against the light coat of sweat on his skin. "There isn't much we can do, Cassidy, unless you've got a snow plough lying around."

"I left it at home." Despite the quip, her voice was hollow. She was tired and cold. It made him feel guilty, though he didn't know what for.

She would have been here even if he hadn't been — and then she would have been alone. She wandered over to the Christmas tree and sat beside it, resting her head against the mirrors. Julian huffed hopelessly and joined her a moment later, their thighs brushing before she shuffled away slightly, as though she couldn't stand his touch. He swallowed down the disappointment.

"Well, it saves us driving back again tomorrow."

It was a joke, but he realized it wasn't funny almost as soon as he said it. If he was honest, he was on the edge of burnout. For the last few weeks, all he had done was think about his routines and catastrophize about what would happen if he didn't get into Phoenix... and if he *did*. If he had to leave his brother. If he had to leave the life he'd known for twenty-four years behind. He couldn't remember the last time he'd done anything to take his mind off things, past taking a twenty-minute shower the other night rather than his usual ten.

"Can I ask you something?" He hadn't meant to say it. Hadn't expected to. But a part of him knew he might not get the chance to talk to her like this again, and he wanted to make the most of what he had. He wanted to understand her better.

"No." That deadpan refusal that she just loved to give him. He had long since stopped listening to it.

"Why did you give it up?"

The question left silence in its wake and he thought he saw Nora wince in his periphery. "You know why."

"Because you choked once." That was putting it politely.

Nora took a ragged breath, fingers peeling away a splinter from the floorboards. In the dim lights, the gold melted her green eyes to silvery, clear lakes, her face all shadows and soft curves. He watched her suck in her bottom lip with more than a little intrigue.

"It sometimes felt more like dancing gave up on me... along with everything else," she answered finally, unable to meet his gaze. "I couldn't be what I was supposed to be."

"And what were you supposed to be?"

"My grandmother, probably."

"Thank God you're not." Julian shuddered at the thought. "That woman has always terrified me. Then again, you have your moments."

"Excuse me," she gaped defensively, "I am nothing like Constance."

"What's that about, anyway? Why do you call her Constance?" Julian couldn't recall a time, even when they were kids, where Nora had ever called her grandmother by anything other than her first name or "Miss Cassidy," like the rest of them — as though Constance had not claimed her as kin. As though she was just another kid in the class.

"What am I supposed to call her?"

"I don't know," Julian shrugged. "Grandma? Nana? Granny?"

"Do you want to try calling Constance 'Granny'?" she shot back.

"Not a chance." He held up his hands in surrender. "But she's not *my* granny. Doesn't she ever treat you like a granddaughter?"

Nora deliberated for a moment. "No. She never acted as anything other than my dance teacher, not even when my dad died."

"She's harsh on you," he noted. The way Constance spoke to Nora was far worse than she would ever dare speak to him — or any of her other students, for that matter. It knocked him sick sometimes just to hear it.

"She's harsh on everybody."

"But she tears you to shreds sometimes. I've heard her." He nudged her with his elbow. "You should stand up to her, you know. You're not the meek little girl you once were. It's high time she realized that, especially if she wants you to take over in her stead."

"It's not worth the earache," she brushed off, clutching the scarf tighter around herself. "Constance only sees what she wants to see, and what she doesn't want to see is me — not as I am, anyway. That's her problem, not mine."

"A part of her must believe in you enough, if she's willing to give you this place."

Nora let out a distorted scoff. "Only because I'm the only Cassidy left and she wants it to stay in the family."

Julian tucked his knees into his chest, the cold beginning to gnaw at him now. It was so quiet in there. So easy to sit beside her now. Despite the discomfort, he didn't want to leave. Where the ice had fallen outside, it had thawed in that room. "What do *you* want?"

Nora's eyes shuttered, staving off any emotion she didn't want him to see. "I don't know."

He knew it was a lie. He had seen what she wanted when she danced and when she taught. Dance still thrummed in her bones and lived in her chest. It still mattered to her.

"You know, my brother loves you. The other teachers never know how to handle him, even at school. They usually push him to one side, tell him to sit out and ignore him. You've never done that, not even when he's difficult."

Finally, she looked at him, and he could breathe again. "He deserves to enjoy dance as much as every other kid in that room. What kind of teacher would I be if I didn't give him that chance?"

Julian's brows lifted in surprise. For a moment, he couldn't find the words, and his throat bobbed as he tried. Then he remembered what it had been like for her growing up. Constance had always pushed her to the back in group pieces. She was always the punching bag, the example given to the rest of the kids of what would happen when they got it wrong the way that she always seemed to do. Even now, it had stuck with her. She had been so insecure in that first rehearsal, hadn't wanted him to so much as touch her — as though she was waiting for him to drop her again or call her names or make fun of her. But Julian wasn't a kid anymore, and he wasn't fickle. He didn't care about her body. It made no difference. When she danced, she was as beautiful as any other performer — if not better, because her passion for it spewed from her with every breath and every beat.

He had moved past it, he realized, but she hadn't. A part of her was still that teenager who had been pushed aside for not fitting in. Just like Fraser.

And he had contributed to those flinches she made when he put his hands on her. He had caused some of it. He understood now why she still hated him so much. Why she had given up. "Dancing gave up on me," she had said, but it hadn't. Everyone else had. In fact, he figured dance was probably the only thing that remained for her, after that competition that had ruined so much.

"You don't want him to be the outcast that you were made to be." There was no question there, because he knew it was true.

The vulnerability that flicked across her features was enough to make Julian ache until she wiped it all away, sniffing as she stood up. "What is this, a therapy session?"

"No, Cassidy." Julian stretched out his legs and yawned, though he did not feel so nonchalant on the inside. "This is a normal conversation between two people. I know you're not used to those."

Nora's rolling eyes felt like a stab to the gut. For a moment, just a moment, he had seen who she was beneath her scorn and irritation... and he liked it.

"Nora." He stopped her as she made to walk away, legs straining as he stood up. "I was a dick growing up."

"'Was'?"

He put his hands on his hips in irritation, his sweater riding up to expose his hips to the cool air. "I'm trying to say I'm sorry, but forget it."

"With pleasure."

Anger surged through him all at once. "You know, you can't blame me for the mistake I made that day forever, and you definitely can't use it as an excuse for giving up. You *chose* to stop dancing, Nora. You *chose* to walk away. I'm sorry for whatever part I played in that, but you need to start accepting that, in the end, it boiled down to you and your insecurities. No one else."

His words seemed not to touch her. She only looked at him with features hewn from impenetrable stone and blinked.

"I'm sleeping in my grandmother's office," she announced, words bathed in vacancy. "Don't bother me until morning."

She left him with his hunched reflection in every mirror as his only companion, shrouded in the shadows and pierced by the sudden draught.

Thirteen

Nora had escaped the studio the next morning before Julian woke up, and things had been tense between them in the two days that followed. After everything he had done, she couldn't believe he'd had the nerve to blame her for all of it — as though he had no idea what damage he and his friends had done to her growing up.

It was easier to ignore him altogether than to try to make him understand, so that was what she had been doing, only talking to him to discuss their next movements for the duet in rehearsals.

The other Walker brother was the one who hovered on the edge of the dance floor today, though. It made a pleasant change, but Fraser's class wasn't until tomorrow, and he was staring absently at the dancers as though he didn't quite know where he was.

Nora left him in peace until her group no longer needed her to teach them the moves and then wandered over as casually as she could so as not to scare him away. "I wasn't expecting to see you here today, buddy."

Fraser said nothing, his glazed almond eyes that were almost identical to Julian's remaining fixed on the dancers as they went over the phrase Nora had just shown them. Nora wondered whether Julian knew his brother was here, or his mother, for that matter. He didn't seem sad or angry, just somewhere else, where Nora couldn't reach. She knew the mood well.

"Is everything okay, Fraser?"

Fraser shrugged. "I wanted to dance."

"Your class is tomorrow," Nora reminded him, casting a hesitant gaze to her dancers. They were intermediate level and all of them were slightly older than Fraser, but she looked at the twelve-year-old, all soft cheeks and tousled hair, and realized it didn't matter. He had come here to dance. Whatever the reason, it was her job to let him. "But if you want to join in at the back, you're more than welcome."

His features lightened with animation. "Really? You'd let me?"

Nora smiled and gave his bony shoulder a gentle squeeze. "Of course. Go join in."

Fraser kicked off his shoes carelessly and joined the back of the class. Nora couldn't help the laughter that built in her throat. She thought about texting Julian, but he would only come and take him home and she didn't want to rip Fraser away from the class if it was helping him now.

The small boy wasn't the best dancer in the world, but his heart was in it. Nora kept an eye on him as she continued with the lesson. Not once did he get frustrated and give up on the more advanced floor work. It was clear from the way his focus never wobbled that he loved to dance and had the potential to be just as good as Julian if he tried hard enough. They were so different, though, Fraser and Julian. His older brother had always been naturally gifted, and that meant he never had to try too hard as a kid, the way that Fraser did now. The way that Nora had. He had let that go to his head, had walked around the studio with his chin stabbing the air and his nose up Constance's ass.

Fraser was his opposite. He didn't care about being good; he only cared about the joy it gave him. He didn't even care about fitting in. He was in his own little bubble, where nothing mattered other than the rhythm he followed. When the other dancers flashed him puzzled looks, earning a disapproving glare from Nora, Fraser didn't even notice.

Had Nora ever felt that way about dance, or had her insecurities plagued her from the moment she took her first step onto the dance floor? She couldn't remember. She wished she could. But dancing with Julian these past few weeks hadn't been like that. Yes, she had been self-conscious to start with and still had her moments, but before the blizzard, it felt as though Nora had shed her old skin and stepped into a new one. She had been enjoying dance, perhaps for the first time, even if it was in short bursts.

It made her want this again. It made her

want to inspire kids like Fraser, let them forge their own path and enjoy every moment of it rather than be restricted by what other people had to say. It made her think for the first time that perhaps she could really do this, really run the studio in Constance's stead and create a safe space for those who needed it.

And then Julian Walker strutted through the door and the idea shattered in her mind. His face was wrought with thunder, but when his eyes fell on Fraser dancing away at the back of the class, he came to a stop. Nora expected him to pull him out, but he didn't. Instead, his posture relaxed.

He made his way over to Nora without lifting his attention from Fraser for a moment.

"I've been looking for him everywhere. Why the hell didn't you text me?"

Nora shrugged and folded her hands behind her back before leaning against the mirror. She tried not to think about the smudged fingerprints she was leaving, for which Constance would scold her later. "I was going to. After the class. Figured he needed the space for a while first."

"It wasn't your decision to make."

Nora sighed, about to point out that Fraser had come to her and not the other way around when she glimpsed his expression. His features were stretched thin, brows knitted together unwaveringly and lines sunk deep into his forehead and around his mouth. His eyes were ablaze with all of the emotion Nora had been searching for in

Fraser. He wasn't even wearing a coat, though it was freezing outside, and she caught the way his shoulders shook — from the chill or his anger, she couldn't tell.

"Did something happen?" she questioned carefully.

"Did he say anything to you?"

"No. He said he just wanted to dance, so I let him join in."

Julian's chest collapsed in relief and he nodded gratefully. "This place is his shelter."

"Shelter from what?"

Bitterness tugged the corner of Julian's mouth down. Finally, he met her eyes, and it was enough to make her want to shrink back, look away. He wasn't okay. She didn't know what to do with that.

"My dad. He's a dick, especially to Fraser. They only see each other twice a week, but it never ends well. I should have been there."

Nora softened in sympathy. With the anguish rolling from Julian, so intense that it had practically turned everything in the studio a dusky red, she couldn't help but put her hand on his arm in comfort. For a moment, she forgot that she hated him and what he'd said to her the other night. She forgot everything, because all she could see was the pain and the rage brewing in the very pits of him, a place she had never seen before. "You're here now."

Julian scoffed but didn't pull away from her

touch. "He'd rather be here with you than come to me. What does that say?"

"He comes here because you inspired him to," she argued gently. "Without you, he wouldn't have this place at all."

Julian opened his mouth to say something, but the music had stopped and the students were waiting expectantly for their dismissal.

"Great job, guys." Nora clapped her hands together and strayed from Julian, though her spine still tingled with the knowledge that he was watching her. "Let's pick it up again next week."

The group filed out except for Fraser, who approached Julian gingerly. In an instant, Julian molded his features into a mask free of worry, so smoothly that he must have done it a thousand times before for Fraser's sake. He beamed at his brother. "How great were you, kiddo?"

Fraser shifted from foot to foot, crossing his arms behind him. "I ran away again."

"I know. It's okay." Hearing the tenderness in Julian's voice, Nora wandered over to the stereo and scrolled through her phone. This moment felt like something only for them and she didn't want to intrude on it. "But next time, you need to tell me or Mom where you're going first, okay? I worry about you."

Fraser nodded hesitantly. "I just wanted to dance. Nora always lets me join in."

A smile curled on her lips and melted when Julian put his hand on Fraser's shoulder, and the boy, for once, did not shy away. "I know."

"You're welcome here anytime, Fraser," she added. "You know that."

Another weak nod. Julian squeezed his brother's shoulder, love flaring in his eyes. Nora had never noticed it glistening there before. It made something painful pull in her chest. "You want to dance for a little bit longer?"

Fraser's face lit up at the offer and he returned to the dance floor without needing to be told twice. Julian slinked over to Nora with his hands in his pockets and his metaphorical tail between his legs. "Thank you for taking care of him."

"It was no problem. Next time, I'll call you right away."

The vow did not set him at ease. He scratched the back of his neck, long sleeves slipping down his arms to reveal translucent skin over green, protruding veins and dark hair. "I've been meaning to talk to you."

"Are you breaking up with me, Julian?" Though it was a taunt, she and he both knew it meant more than that. It meant things were okay. They could slip back into teasing one another, hating one another, even, without the heaviness of Julian's words weighing them down. She didn't know how she managed it, only that she wanted to. For the first time, she did not just see him as the stone cold, arrogant boy who had let her fall off the stage five years ago. He was a concerned brother and a hopeful dancer, desperate for the chance at success. He was her dance partner. He was the guy who had fixed up her car without her asking. He was....

Nora didn't know what he was anymore. She didn't know much of anything as she waited for his reply, realizing that, for once, she could not even begin to know what would come out of his mouth. It used to be guaranteed mockery. Now, it might have been anything.

"Funny," he responded humorlessly. "I want to apologize to you, properly this time. Will you let me?"

Her stomach coiled and uncoiled restlessly. She didn't need his apology or his pity. She didn't need anything from him. It was enough to know that he cared enough to try. "No apology necessary. It's forgotten."

Doubt fluttered across his features. "Is it?"

"Julian." She blew out a sharp breath. "You and I hate each other. We always will. Let's just get on with the dance and stop letting all that get in the way. The sooner we do, the sooner we're done with each other for good. Yes?"

Julian raised his brows in surprise, a subdued chuckle catching in his throat. "Ouch. Don't mince your words on my account."

"Am I wrong?" Nora put her hands on her hips, waiting. Hoping, perhaps, that he would argue, tell her it wasn't like that between them anymore.

But he didn't.

"No, I guess not," he said, face falling. The absence of his gaze when he returned his focus to Fraser left her cold. "Let's go, kiddo."

Nora remained frozen as Julian dragged his brother out without another word. She had thought that finally simplifying things and putting everything out in the open would make things easier to handle between them and prevent her from getting hurt.

Instead, she only felt more confused.

Fourteen

The dance was almost finished. As though sensing it like a grey-haired, sour-faced shark catching the scent of blood, Constance had been hovering around the studio all morning. Her presence had been a phantom one over the last two weeks. She seemed to be coming into the studio less and less, a fact that Nora did not mind too much since it meant she was not being perpetually heckled by her demands and criticisms. That day, though, the peace was shattered.

Dripping with sweat, Nora had been about to strip off her sweater and dance in only her leotard and tights, but that ship sailed quickly when Constance dragged a chair onto the floor, legs scraping against wood, and sat without invitation in the middle of the practice. The last thing Nora needed was to have her body ridiculed again.

Julian pretended to ignore the old woman. Nora couldn't. She glanced at Constance expectantly, pulling the slackened strap of her sports bra back onto her shoulder. Without really looking in the mirrors behind, she knew she was a mess, tomato-faced and hair escaping its braid. Since they were almost done, they were working harder than ever before, and more choreography meant more stamina was needed to sustain them through it. Her legs were slowly dissolving into jelly, heart ricocheting against her ribs. It had been a long time since she'd last worked this hard, if ever.

"I'd like to see it," Constance demanded once she was sure they had both noticed her sitting there.

"It's not finished," Nora protested, using her sleeve to smear away the beads of sweat that gleamed in her hairline. "We have about thirty seconds left yet."

"I'd like to see it," Constance repeated, sitting back in her chair so she could look down, past her glasses and her nose, on them both. "Perhaps I can help."

"Next week—" Nora began to suggest but was cut off before she could.

"I'd like to see it now." A cool, bitter smile twisted itself onto her thin lips, as though she knew exactly what she was doing and enjoyed every moment of it. Constance often got into moods like these, moods where cruelty was embedded in her every move and every gesture. Nora had borne the brunt of them more than enough times growing up. Icy dread swished around her stomach as she shot Julian a pleading look.

But Julian was Miss Cassidy's favorite, and he wouldn't disappoint her. He nodded in agreement, straightening out the curtain they had been wrangling around all morning. "Alright. Let's take it from the top."

"Julian—"

"I certainly hope, child, that you are not holding Mr. Walker back in his practices," Constance announced over Nora's attempted objection.

Nora sighed and flashed a grim smile, pressing "play" on the music player before taking her position behind the curtain.

It was probably the best she had danced in a long time — the best they had danced together, too. Without looking, she could feel them synchronizing with each breath of unison, each extension pulling her body so tight that not one part of her remained still or disused. She didn't stumble when Julian flung her around, nor did he when she leapt onto him from behind. He grounded her. She grounded him. Everything they had been working on finally felt worth it... until they finished and Nora stopped the music, chest heaving desperately for air. Constance's face had not twitched an inch since they had begun, as though they hadn't danced at all.

She turned to Julian first. "Your lines were lovely, Mr. Walker. Your intensity, too, and the choreography is exceptional. Phoenix would be lucky to have you."

"Thank you, Miss Cassidy," Julian grinned tautly, cheeks dimpling. His own forehead was damp with sweat, cheeks flushed a pale pink, and his deep brown hair had fallen into his eyes. He apparently hadn't found it necessary to mention that Nora had choreographed at least half of the dance, if not more, and the fact made Nora's blood boil.

She tried not to flinch when the attention turned to her.

"Nora, I wish I could say the same for you."

She wanted to throw up. Acid burned her throat, her breath escaping in jagged, shallow gasps as she waited for ultimate destruction.

"Your feet were sickled. Your jetés were lazy. Your arms lacked purpose. When you chasséd into the corner in the first sequence, you sounded like an elephant bounding across the floor. You had all of the grace of one, too." They kept coming, each criticism more personal and more painful than the last. Nora could only stand and take it, the way she always had before. This was exactly why she had quit. This was everything she hated about dance. "You looked like an amateur in comparison to your partner. If you want to run this studio, you are going to have to do better than that. *Much* better."

Constance left the two of them in the ashes of her blistering wake, heading into her office and slamming the door with finality. Somehow, the silence that followed did not serve as a comfort. Nora swallowed the lump in her throat, but it did her no good. Her eyes were already swimming with tears, and there was no way to stop them from rolling down her pink-stained cheeks. She turned her back to Julian, forgetting that there were mirrors on every wall and he could see her just as well no matter where she stood.

"Cassidy—"

"Don't." She shook her head at the crack in her own voice. *Pathetic*. She was a grown adult, crying because her grandmother still enjoyed making her feel small. But she had thought she was doing better, thought that she had danced well. She had thought she could do this.

Julian let out a strained, uneasy huff, his leg shaking uncomfortably as though he wasn't sure if he should go to her.

Nora saved him from the internal battle and left without another word.

It took Julian about two seconds to follow his unsettled gut and knock on Constance's door. He was surprised to find that his own fists shook with anger as he rapped on the wood — his whole body, actually. Nora was a *good* dancer. He had *never* seen her dance with sickled feet in all of their years together — if anything, she even walked with a turn-out. Her grandmother was a bully, and he was too old to sit by and watch because he was afraid of standing up to her.

"Come in," Constance called frostily from the other side of the door.

He did, flinging the door open with enough force that Constance lifted her glassy eyes from her paperwork. "Mr. Walker. How can I help you?"

"You can start by stopping whatever that was." It was an effort just to keep his voice steady. The last thing he wanted to do was yell at an old woman, no matter how vicious she was.

"I'm not sure what you're referring to," she dismissed with a wave of her liver-spotted hand.

"That," he pointed behind him, to the studio, "with Nora. With all due respect, Miss Cassidy, what you said was completely unfair. Nora has worked hard on this dance. She came up with most of the choreography herself. I don't see why you tore her down that way. We were good, and you know it."

"Nora is a big girl," Constance replied, apathy turning her words stiff. "If she has a problem with my feedback, she can come to me herself, Mr. Walker."

"That wasn't feedback, Miss Cassidy." He shook his head, understanding for the first time why Nora had given up dance — and how it could have given up on her. It wasn't dance itself that had hurt her badly enough that she had walked away; it was the monster in front of him, whispering in her ear, telling her she would never be good enough. All of the times she had flinched away from him, all of the ways she had tried to tell him, and he hadn't listened. He hadn't understood how bad it was. This wasn't just nitpicking. It was something that had ripped into every fiber of her being and made a poisonous little home for itself there. It should have ruined her. Constance was just like his father, and he hated her for it. "That was ripping your granddaughter to shreds without reason. I can't change the way you are with her, but if you want to do it, do it in your own time, not mine. I'd imagine the last thing you'd want is for me to cut connections with Cassidy's School of Dance right before I join a renowned company. It wouldn't be good for business, would it?"

The threat seemed to shock Julian more than Constance. In fact, she seemed proud of his venom. It only made him feel worse and he fought the urge to continue with it by drinking in a long breath.

"You would be harming your partner more than me, Mr. Walker. I won't be around for much longer."

Julian glowered with resignation, knowing it was true. If Constance was retiring, nothing he could do would affect her.

"Then I'll ask you kindly, Miss Cassidy," he forced out through bared teeth. "You proposed the idea of us dancing together. You wanted this for her. Let her have it without breaking her in the process."

"If I was capable of breaking her, she would have been broken long ago."

"And yet you keep trying. Why?"

Constance straightened in her chair. "I prepare her for what is to come. I have spent my whole life molding her into somebody with strength and resilience so that she will not be so surprised when she finds that others are not so kind about a dancer of her... build."

Julian grimaced. He had seen the broken pieces that Constance had left, shattered on the dance floor. He had seen Nora pick them up and glue them back together before and after she had walked away. It might have made her stronger, just as his own father's torment had taught him to stand up for himself, but there would always be a weakness, a cavity that ate away at her because of it. Family seemed to have a way of drilling holes that were not so easily filled. The very idea that Constance thought she was helping Nora....

"You belittle her. You make her feel un- worthy. You humiliate her. She deserves better than that. Better than you."

For once, Constance had no vile retort or stony glare. Her mouth opened. Shut.

Julian took advantage of her speechless- ness, gripping the chair in front of him with rigid hands. "I'll only ask once, Miss Cassidy. Don't *ever* use Nora as your personal punching bag again. She's not a kid anymore, and she shouldn't have to feel like one so you can keep walking around this place with your nose in the air. I appreciate the help you've given me, but lay off."

He left it at that, though he could have spoken for hours more about his contempt for the trick Constance had pulled tonight. He didn't want to be stuck in that office a moment longer. Cassidy was out there somewhere, destroyed, and the ache in his heart whispered to him to go to her.

He would listen.

Fifteen

Everything was stained blue outside. Snow had fallen thinly across the parking lot — was still falling, actually, in a light dusting that tickled Julian's skin as he stepped out. He was glad to find Nora's car was still parked. As he approached, he could just make out her silhouette behind the steering wheel.

He swallowed down his own anger and regret as he tapped on the window. Standing up to Constance that way would probably come back to bite him. God only knows what Nora would think of it… if he ever told her.

"Is there room for one more in there, Cassidy?"

"No." Even as she said it, voice muffled by the glass, she huffed and opened the door for him. He grinned in amusement and slid in beside her. Her eyes were red-rimmed and her cheeks tear-stained, but the crying had stopped, thank God. Still, he had never seen her this deflated. She wouldn't look at him, and he wouldn't force her. Instead, they sat suspended in silence for a moment, watching the white specks float down onto the car. Nora warmed her trembling hands by the growling heater that was their only soundtrack.

He didn't know what to say. He couldn't ask if she was okay because he already knew the answer. Nobody would be okay after being taken down that way by their own grandmother, and this hadn't even been a one off. She had been treated this way her whole life.

"For what it's worth, your grandmother talks shit."

Nora rolled her eyes and pressed her head against the window, sniffling. "Don't let Miss Cassidy hear you talk like that. You won't be her favorite anymore."

"That ship has well and truly sailed," he murmured. "You know that none of what she said in there is true, don't you?"

"Julian," she sighed, voice thick with exhaustion, "you don't have to do this. I'm fine. I'm a big girl now. I'm used to this."

"You shouldn't be," he shot back. "It's wrong, the way she treats you. The way we all treated you as kids. And it's not true: I would be fucked without you and your choreography."

"Please," she scoffed. "If Sienna had stayed —"

The name didn't hurt him to hear the way he had thought it would. In fact, she hadn't crossed his mind at all for weeks now. They hadn't even said a proper goodbye, had left it the way it was outside of the studio, and it didn't bother him at all.

"If Sienna was here, we'd spit out the same old tired lifts and motifs we've been doing since we were ten. You... Nora, you've made me a better dancer. Don't get me wrong, you're a complete pain in my ass, but you challenge me in ways nobody else could. We've got something good here, and I know it, and I think you know it, too. Your grandmother... she wouldn't know good if it hit her in the face."

She rested her head against the window. Each second she spent letting his words sink in was one where Julian felt more stupid than the last for being so honest.

Finally, she looked at him. "Are you just saying this because you're worried I'll quit on you?"

"You're not going to quit on me, Cassidy," he said with an edge of certainty. "You're too stubborn for that."

To his surprise, the corner of her mouth twitched. She knew he was right. If she was going to quit, she wouldn't have stayed and waited for him. They had come too far now to go back. The dance was almost done. In little over a month, it would be over.

The thought didn't bring the relief Julian thought it would.

"Always so cocky," she murmured, playing with the frayed edges of her scarf. Julian fought the urge to reach out and steady that shaking hand, feel its warmth from the heater, and comfort her in ways that words wouldn't. Even though she had calmed down and the tears had fled, he could see the sadness beneath her smile, and he wished more than anything he could demolish it until it was nothing but dust.

"Am I wrong?"

"No," she agreed. "You're not wrong. I'm going to prove her wrong, Julian. I'm going to prove them all wrong."

Pride swelled in him.

"I know." He opened the door and climbed out. "Come on. Swap."

"Why?"

He ducked his head back to the window so he could still see her. "We need a break from this place. Let's go somewhere."

"You think you're driving my car?"

"I drove your car after I fixed it, and it turned out fine, didn't it?" he reasoned, and then, because she had not moved, he opened her door and exposed her to the cold. "Come on. Let's go."

Nora groaned but obeyed, shimmying into the passenger seat to make room for him. "And where are we going to go in the dark and the cold?"

Julian sat and pulled his seat belt across himself. "Anywhere but here."

Sixteen

The sun had set, leaving the woods pitch black, save for Julian's headlights spilling across the untouched snow. Nora had suspected some kind of detour to one of the old pizza places on the edge of town, so when they rolled to a stop with nothing but the tangle of skeletal branches sinking beneath the snow's weight to point to where they were, Nora frowned and sat up a little straighter.

"Is this where you're going to murder me and bury my body?"

"Not yet. I had that planned for *after* the showcase, but you weren't supposed to find out." Julian turned off the engine but kept the headlights lit. He let out a sigh, looking out at the view in front of them. "I used to do what Fraser did and run off every time I had a blow up with my dad. Only I didn't always go to the studio. Sometimes, I came here."

Reluctantly, Nora freed herself from her seat belt. "And do what?"

Julian shrugged, his long fingers tapping out an indecipherable rhythm on the steering wheel. "Sit. Dance. Cry. Shout. Sing. Whatever I felt like. We all need a safe place, right?"

"Right," Nora nodded, her surprise leaving her unable to string a sentence together. The last person she'd expected to understand that was him.

"I'll let you share mine, as long as you don't tell anybody else about it."

"Generous," she acknowledged. And then, softer, "Your secret's safe with me."

"So, shall we?" He tilted his head in question.

"What?"

"Dance."

Nora almost let out a laugh of disbelief. "It's snowing, and it's freezing."

"Well, I'm going to dance." The corners of his mouth lifted as he turned on his stereo. A soft, low song floated out a moment later, wrapping Nora in the warmth the male vocals provided. He cranked it up until it pierced her ears and then got out, leaving his door open as he stood in the headlights and squinted.

Nora huffed and followed him hesitantly, the damp snow seeping through her shoes and straight into her socks. It rasped beneath her as her footprints stained the white sheet in a way that felt gratifying, as though it wanted to remember her. Them.

Her breath fogged in front of her and she tucked her arms around herself to shield herself from the sudden change in temperature. "What are we going to do, just pretend we have the props?"

Julian grinned, tongue swiping across his teeth in amusement. "We're not doing that dance tonight, Cassidy."

"Then what are we doing?"

He shrugged. "Anything we want. Let's see how well we improvise together."

Nora worked hard to keep her expression neutral as he took her hand and began to sway. Behind them, the pines creaked and groaned as light flakes of snow floated down. They clung to Julian's dark hair, making their home on his shoulders and leaving glistening droplets freckled across his skin. He tilted his head up to catch them in his mouth, tongue curling to his chin. Nora couldn't help but laugh at the immaturity of it, but then she did the same, the snow a sharp freshness that dissolved on her tongue and tasted like a winter night.

"I don't think this should go in the routine," Julian spoke, mouth still wide open. Then, he looked down at Nora again. She had never seen him the way he was now, eyes dancing with light and skin glowing. Happy. He was happy.

And she was with him to see it.

Nora licked her cracked lips, cheeks aching with her smile. Julian returned it with his own and then twirled her around. Laughing, she stumbled into his chest, fingers clenching against his fleece jacket. Her untamed hair whipped around with her and fell across her face. Noticing, he tilted her chin up and brushed it away, his touch nothing more than a delicate graze against her icy skin. They were so close that his warm breath fanned across Nora's face. His other arm curled low around her back.

To avoid looking at him, she arched her back until the world was upside down. Julian's hands slid to her waist to keep her steady, and then they were dancing across her spine, into her hair, as she curled back up before falling into her next movement. He followed her, their arms a tangle of bones and sharp joints and their bodies never breaking contact for more than a moment. They moved to the beat of the song, the woods their new dance floor. He knew each move she would make before she did, and she knew his. Their bundled layers were no restriction. It wasn't their movements, their leg lines or their leaps, that they cared about. It was what they were expressing through them, things they were too afraid to express anywhere else. White powder flicked up with their feet, disrupting the well-ironed quilt of fresh snow and leaving behind smeared imprints of movement and stony mounds of sludge.

They were one being, one entity, carving lines into the world as the headlights flooded them in silvery light.

They were magic.

They ended with Nora's knee drawn up to his waist, panting breaths blowing the hair from her face and her chest throbbing against his torso. It was silent as the song faded and the next one began, leaving them completely alone and completely still, save for their ragged breathing.

"Julian," she whispered, for lack of anything else to say.

His fingers bunched in her leggings as his grip tightened, his other hand knotting into her hair. So close. They were so close, her breasts flush against him. Her nipples peaked and she thanked the heavens she was wearing enough layers he wouldn't notice.

Still, as though sensing it, his lips grazed across her forehead and then fell down to her nose. She wanted to pull away. She wanted him to kiss her.

"What are you doing?" she breathed, still unable to free herself of him. Her calf burned as she balanced on it.

Corded muscle tensed beneath her hands, and his throat bobbed as he swallowed. "I don't know."

Finally, his clutch loosened and she put her leg down slowly. Still, they did not cleave apart. They stood close enough that their hips touched and heat coiled in her stomach. This was not the Julian Walker who had dropped her all those years ago. This was the Julian Walker who took care of his brother, vowed never to drop her, fixed up her car because he knew what it meant to her, and danced with her in the snow.

But he was also the Julian Walker who had blamed Nora for her own insecurities. She had forgotten for a moment who he was, how he could hurt her so easily when he tried. She stepped away, scraping the damp hair from her eyes. Her eyelashes caught snowflakes and she blinked them away in irritation.

"It's getting cold. We should go."

"Nora." Her heart fluttered when he said her name like that, with no sarcasm dripping from it: just her first name, as though he only ever meant the things he said when he called her "Nora" and not "Cassidy." As though it meant this, now, was real, and all that had come before was just a game. "I know you don't trust me—"

"Can we not do this?" she pleaded, teeth chattering. "We have just over a month until the Winter Showcase and then we don't have to put up with each other anymore. Let's just stay focused, okay?"

His expression fell, jaw clenching, but he nodded and sucked in a breath. "If that's what you want."

"It is," Nora said and prayed that Julian couldn't hear the lie in her words. She had never expected to be here with him, feeling this way. She hated him. She hated everything he had ever done to get her here. She hated the way he used to sit and watch the other kids taunt her and the way he hadn't bothered to catch her the way he was supposed to at the competition. She hated how infuriatingly arrogant he had always been and how he had forced her to do this along with her grandmother.

She hated that he was standing pathetically in front of her now, with his hair dripping and his mouth downturned, as though *she* was the one hurting *him*. As though he cared.

Finally, his eyes turned cold, and he looked away.

"Alright," he muttered, throwing himself into the driver's seat and turning off the radio. Without the wavering harmonies, everything felt hollow. "Let's go, Cassidy."

Seventeen

Julian waited in his car to take Fraser home after his dance lesson. He had a rehearsal with Nora that night, but until then, he couldn't face her — or Constance, if she had decided to show her face after last night. Everything was too confusing, too broken. It had been easier to hate Nora than want to kiss her and protect her and….

He closed his eyes before he could finish the train of thought, head sinking into the back of his seat as the same song they had improvised to in the snow last night floated out of his stereo. He had never danced like that before with anyone. He had never felt so in sync, so connected to another human being. It had just worked. *They* had just worked. And yet Nora still hated him, that much was clear in the way she pulled away, left him wanting something he could never have — and he couldn't blame her.

He shouldn't have even been focused on that. His callback with Phoenix was the next day, and surely, that mattered more. The nerves buzzing just beneath his skin told him so.

A forceful rapping on the window broke him away from it all. He half expected to open his eyes and find Nora standing there, with her arms crossed or hands on her hips, as they usually were. Instead, a face that did not belong anywhere near this studio glowered back at him, leathery and wrinkled with distaste. His father.

Julian's heart nearly dropped out of his ass. He rolled his window down slowly, buying time. "Dad. What are you doing here?"

"What are *you* doing here?" he bit back with a vicious jab through the crack in the window. His hands were still blackened with their usual grease. "Where the hell is your brother?"

Hesitating, Julian glanced to the studio. A lie. He needed a lie to get him through this. If Graham knew that Fraser was dancing in there... it wouldn't end well.

"You told me you were taking him to see a movie today," Graham accused, dark eyes blazing as he glanced between Julian and the dance studio. "You lying bastard. You brought him *here*?"

"No," Julian said quickly. "I dropped him off at a friend's house."

Graham scoffed and Julian knew his mistake. "Fraser doesn't have any damn friends. You go and get him out of there, *now*, or I will. I won't have another prima ballerina in place of a son."

"Dad," Julian pleaded, the car door nudging Graham away as he got out warily. "He likes dancing. There's nothing wrong with that."

"Is this your mother's doing?" Graham spat. The way his lip curled, revealing a set of yellowed, crooked teeth that Julian had been lucky not to inherit made him sick to his stomach. "Does she know about this?"

"Of course, she knows," Julian replied. "She wanted him to do something he enjoyed. It helps him, Dad."

"Bullshit." Graham trembled with anger, pulling up his loose jeans as he turned away and marched toward the studio. Julian followed, trying desperately to pull him back, but after four decades of fixing broken cars and hauling around heavy parts, his father was far stronger.

The door to the studio nearly shattered when Graham swung it open. Immediately, the class turned to stare at the sudden interruption. Nora stood mid-plié with her hand resting against the ballet barre at the front, frozen.

Julian's entire body burned with embarrassment, but that didn't matter. What mattered was the harm this would do to his brother.

"Fraser," Graham rasped out, searching the rows of students for his son.

"Dad, get out," Julian ordered, trying to push him back outside. Graham dodged him, dirtied boots treading mud onto the floorboards as he continued.

"Fraser. Now."

Fraser's dark curls popped up over a sea of heads, his eyes wide with bewilderment. His face paled when he caught sight of his father and Julian trying in vain to get rid of him.

"Mr. Hart." Nora weaved through her students and took up a protective stance in front of them. Out of everybody — besides Fraser, of course — she was the one who Julian least wanted here to witness this terrible mess. "Is there a problem?"

"The problem," Graham bit through gritted teeth, "is that I didn't consent to my son taking dance classes. I'll be taking him home now."

"With all due respect, Mr. Hart, Fraser's mother has paid for a month's worth of classes." Nora didn't waver as she spoke, a fact that Julian would have admired if he wasn't so anxious. "You can take him home when his lesson has ended."

Graham's face twisted into a sneer. "And who are you to tell me what I can and can't do with my son?"

"Dad—" Julian begged, urging him back. Graham didn't budge, did not so much as even glance at Julian.

"I'm his dance teacher, sir," Nora replied calmly. Julian could see the anger blazing beneath the façade, though, and the slight tremble of her fingers as she crossed her hands over her torso. "And I don't take well to people interrupting my lessons. If you could please wait outside—"

"Fraser, I mean it," Graham warned, barging past Nora. Fraser lingered on the edge of the group, tears gathering in his eyes. It broke Julian's heart. What was worse was that he could do nothing to stop this. He had failed him, with no idea how it had even come to this. "Come on. We're going home."

The commotion had dragged Constance out from her office. She seemed bedraggled, her white, wiry hair loose from its usual tight bun.

"Dad, I swear to God—" Julian began.

"Fraser, stay where you are," Nora demanded, stepping in front of him as her voice rose with authority. "Mr. Hart, you're embarrassing yourself, you're upsetting your son, and you are scaring my students. Please wait outside."

"Don't tell me what to do." Graham pointed a vicious finger into Nora's chest. Julian nearly growled in threat, gripping his father's arms behind his back so he could go no further. "You think because you're fucking around with my princess of a son, you have a right to tell me how to be a parent? I don't think so."

"Have some decorum. There are children here," Nora snarled in reply. Julian nearly flinched with the rage simmering there. "I don't know why you think your behaviour is okay, but while they're here, you will not belittle your sons and you certainly will not belittle me. Any other parent would be bursting with pride of the things Julian and Fraser are accomplishing. You're just a bully and a coward and there's no place for that here. I won't ask you again, Mr. Hart. Get out of my studio."

Julian could do nothing but stare in awe, but Graham remained unfazed. He brushed past Nora again and grabbed Fraser by the arm, dragging him out as he fought desperately to stay.

Julian shook his head in disgust and followed them.

"It's okay, Fraser," was all he could say — it wasn't enough. He knew that as he glanced back at Nora and saw her standing, heartbroken, with her hand on her chest. The class staring behind her. Constance, too, had not moved from her spot by the corridor. "I'm sorry for the disruption."

Behind him, Graham hauled his son right out of the dance studio, and not one person there could stop him. Not even Julian.

Eighteen

Nora didn't know what to say when Julian turned up that evening, disheveled and slumped and nothing like the man she had gotten to know these past weeks. It made it worse knowing his audition was tomorrow and it was bound to be playing on his mind, along with everything else.

The studio had cleared out. Even Constance had left after the incident, claiming that it had been enough drama for her today. Nora, for once, was inclined to agree with her.

"I'm sorry," she said finally, approaching him with careful steps. "I'm so sorry, Julian. I had no idea."

"It wasn't your fault, Cassidy." He was trying to keep his tone light for her, but sadness teetered on the edge of his smile and at the creases in the corner of his eyes. He was shattered. Guilty. Devastated. Nora could only imagine how Fraser felt. "You couldn't have known."

"How's Fraser?" She'd been worrying about him all afternoon, chest aching with the memory of how he'd fought as his father forced him out.

"He's at my mom's, now." Exhaustion seeped through every word as he shrugged off his coat and hung it up. "He'll be okay. She's dealing with it."

Without thinking, Nora slung her arms around him as though he had pulled her in by a piece of string and wrapped him up as though she could protect him from all that she had seen today. Everything made sense now: why he was so desperate to get into Phoenix, why he had always been so uptight about dancing. Maybe even why he had always followed in Constance's footsteps. He had his own bully at home, just as Nora had hers, but while hers was all barbed insults veiled as constructive criticism, his was brute force he could not be shielded from.

Julian tensed against her at first and then relaxed a moment later, a deep inhale bubbling beneath her as he caught his breath. "Thank you for having Fraser's back. What you said, the way you stood up to him... it meant a lot to me."

"Of course," she whispered, her eyes fluttering closed as his fingers locked in her hair. Remembering the almost kiss last night, a ghost of the flame she had felt in her stomach returned and Nora pulled away from him. "Is there anything else I can do?"

He shook his head, sagging again, as though trying to sink into the floorboards beneath him. "You've done more than enough."

Nora sighed solemnly, searching his face for some hint as to how she could help. Her incessant need to fix things was becoming quite an annoyance. Still, she caught a glimpse of the Christmas tree in the corner and remembered how they had talked that night of the blizzard, before Julian had said all of the wrong things. She had turned the lights off earlier and danced. Maybe Julian wanted the same.

She turned out the main lights, leaving the room lit in the dim, golden glow. Julian's brows knitted together in curiosity. "Nora, my audition is tomorrow—"

"I know." She shrugged and dragged him to sit beside the tree, mirrors of who they had been only a few weeks ago. "And we'll work on your solo in a few minutes. But let's just stop for a second. You look exhausted."

Julian's lids shuttered and he rubbed his hands across his face roughly. "I am."

"Was your dad like that when you were growing up, too?" she dared ask. She could remember his mother at the competitions, once or twice, but never the dark, broad man who had barged through her studio and almost tore through the wooden floorboards today.

Julian nodded. "Charming, isn't he?"

"How did you deal with it?"

"The same way you dealt with Constance, probably," he offered. "Buried all that lovely childhood trauma and kept going."

Nora hummed, stretching her legs out in front of her and crossing them.

"Fraser, though…" he continued, and the

way his words seemed to come out blistered and burnt made her heart shatter. "He's different. He can't deal with it the same way I can. I worry about what will happen if I'm not here anymore. He has my mom, but she can't always protect him from my dad. Maybe... maybe I shouldn't leave him. Maybe all of this was a mistake."

On instinct, Nora took his hand and planted it in her lap. Their fingers laced together, pale skin against dark, soft flesh against hard stone. "Your brother looks up to you. He needs you to show him that it's okay to be exactly who you are, to chase your dreams no matter who tries to take him from you." She waited for him to comment on the corniness, but he seemed to be hanging onto every word as though he had never been comforted before. Maybe he hadn't. She didn't know much about his relationship with Sienna, and his mother was a businesswoman who had barely ever made it to competitions. It had always been the two of them at the back of the coach, alone. Only Julian had friends who he had gradually gravitated toward, whereas Nora never moved forward. "You'd be doing a disservice to him and yourself if you let your father ruin everything now."

"And what about my brother?" Julian's voice cracked. "What will happen to him if I'm not there to look out for him?"

"I can help with that," Nora shrugged. "I can check up on him. Between me and your mother, he'll be supported. I promise."

"Why?"

Nora glanced at him in question.

"Why would you help me?"

"Because if I can't use this studio to help people, what's the point?" she replied. "And because you might be a complete prick, Julian Walker, but nobody deserves to deal with what you had to today. I meant what I said. You and Fraser deserve better than that."

"I wish I could go back to that competition." The truth of his words came out raw and scratchy and weak, they took Nora aback enough that her breath hitched and her stomach flipped. "I wish I could change the way it went. Because if I had the chance to do it again, I'd catch you, Nora. I'd catch you every time."

"Do you mean that?" she breathed, gulping.

"I do."

Nora hated that, for the first time, she trusted his word completely.

Nineteen

Julian paced the halls of the theatre, a scramble of nerves and electricity knotting itself in his stomach. Nora sat still enough for the both of them on the empty bench by the wall, car keys clenched in her hand. She had offered to take him to the call back and he hadn't been too proud to decline. He didn't want to be alone in this anymore. Her being here... it meant something to him.

He cracked his knuckles and shook the cold from his toes, not for the first time.

"Julian Walker, nervous," Nora observed smugly, lips twitching in amusement. Things weren't strange between them despite everything that had changed. With the new day had come the same old sarcasm and teasing they'd always shared, if not slightly diluted now — enough that she was closer to a friend than an enemy. Which was good. A friend was what he needed her to be. Nothing more... or so he told himself. "I never thought I'd see the day."

"Can you at least pretend you're not enjoying it?" Julian narrowed his eyes as he bounced on the balls of his feet, letting out a puff of breath and running through the choreography in his head

again. There would be more than just one performance today. They wanted him to tackle their own
sequence. He'd been learning it along with his own
short solo since his first audition.

"No," she replied with a grin. "And you're
going to tread a hole in the floor if you don't stand
still."

It dawned on him that she was distracting
him to calm him down, teasing him as though
everything was normal and his entire future didn't
rest on the next hour. He shook his head but sat beside her, his thigh brushing hers as he bounced his
leg.

"At least I don't have to dance with you
today," he pointed out. "No constant moaning for
a sip of water or sweaty hands on my back every
time I lift you."

"You'll miss all of that, really." Her green
eyes glittered in amusement. He got caught in
them for a moment, bound by the brown flecks
he'd never noticed before and the way they locked
on him without fear.

"I will," he allowed himself to admit softly.

Nora broke their gaze first, patting him on
the shoulder with icy hands that made him recoil.
"Just don't forget me when you're a star."

Julian scoffed. "I couldn't forget you if I
tried, Cassidy — and believe me, I've tried."

"Julian Walker?" an assertive voice called
his name. A small woman wearing a polo shirt and
holding a clipboard stood at the end of the corri-

dor, waiting.

Swallowing down the last of his nerves, he stood on trembling knees. Nora followed him, fingers curling around his wrist. "Good luck. You got this."

He softened in appreciation, wishing just for a moment that she was in his arms again. Wishing she could come with him, dance with him, so he wouldn't have to stand in that darkness alone.

She couldn't, though, so he stepped away with a lingering gaze, memorizing the pink of her lips and the way her hair curled around her round cheeks before he plunged into the unknown lying before him.

∞∞∞

The spotlight blinded him. The rest of the auditorium was bathed in a blackness Julian was grateful for. He could just about make out Jennifer sitting with a man on one side of her and a woman who looked remarkably like her on the other. Jennifer's fingers were curled around her pen, her expression warm and welcoming as Julian padded onto the stage barefoot.

"Good to see you again, Julian." She nodded as though they had been friends for years.

Julian shot his widest grin back, rolling his shoulders and keeping his posture as straight as he could. "And you, Miss Phoenix."

"How's the duet coming along?"

"Perfect," he said, and it didn't feel like a lie. It felt as though Nora and Julian had finally crossed a barrier with the duet. They were comfortable with each other, no longer afraid to linger in moments when they were supposed to and reach for one another with everything they had. The night they had improvised in the snow had morphed them from dancers forced together to partners who knew one another like the backs of their hands. "I'm eager for you to see the piece."

"As am I," Jennifer agreed. "We'll see your own solo first, please. When you're ready."

Julian took up his position, fighting to keep his heart from slipping straight out of his rib cage and onto the shiny stage. He imagined Nora watching him from the wings, whispering the movements in his ear and telling him to keep his focus. He remembered dancing with only the Christmas lights washing over him and the way her own face had reflected that mellow, golden glow back as she suggested new ideas and supported him, even when she didn't have to. He remembered how it had felt like home and pretended that was where he was now. With her.

That was how, when the music began to play, he didn't stumble or falter. Every step as precise as the last, every split and leap and slide as smooth as butter. The music lived in his bones with him, told him to curve and sway and pirouette as though it was his own breath. He didn't dance just for himself anymore.

He danced for her, too.

∞∞∞

"Well?" Nora pounced on Julian as soon as he emerged, breathless and sweaty, from the theater.

When he broke out of his post-dancing haze enough to notice her standing by her car, a grin illuminated his face. "Perfect. Couldn't have gone better."

Before she could clap and praise him, his hands had wrapped around her waist and he was twirling her around as though she was light as a feather. She didn't balk or shy away the way she once might have. She knew he could bear her weight. Knew he wouldn't drop her.

She laughed out his name like a song, kicking until he finally put her down.

"Now your sweat is all over me. Disgusting."

"I don't care," he chuckled, his touch lingering on her hips. "I think I actually have a real chance at this, Nora. I could be a dancer. A real dancer. I could get out of this town for good."

She beamed brightly and let him hug her again, his breath whispering through her hair with the wind, but she couldn't ignore the ache in her chest. He was so eager to leave it all behind… to leave *her* behind. It had always been inevitable, but they had just started to get used to one another, and soon, he would be gone for good.

"Well, Jennifer Phoenix would be a fool if she didn't take you with her."

"You're just looking forward to getting rid of me, Cassidy," he quipped, sharp jaw brushing her cheek as he pulled away. She savored the last of his warmth as he led her away with his arm around her. For a moment, she caught their reflection in the glossy side of her car and didn't see a dumpy girl filled with decade-old spite for the perfect man standing beside her. She saw two dance partners, comfortable and close and not even a little bit mismatched. Because their partnership made sense to her now.

Because, she found, she no longer hated Julian Walker — and that terrified her right down to her bones.

Twenty

"I was thinking," Julian said through gasps of breath as Nora turned off the music. She had thought Julian would want a break after his audition, but she was wrong. He had dragged her here after getting lunch in town, as though he wanted her to have indigestion with all of the pasta churning in her stomach.

"Uh oh," Nora replied, eyebrows flicking up. "That's never a good sign."

He cast her an unamused look before continuing. "I was thinking we could fit a small solo in the middle."

"You have a solo in already," she countered, trying not to stare too long at the flash of well-toned abs Julian revealed as he wiped sweat off his face with the hem of his shirt. Every time she looked at him these days, he seemed to get more beautiful, and she was reminded of how close they had been to kissing that night in the snow. It was becoming inconvenient. Standing beside a talented and golden god wasn't great for her self-esteem... or that strange, light fluttering in her stomach that had once been a gnawing, heavy hatred.

Things had changed between them. She didn't know yet if it was for the better.

"I mean a solo for you."

Nora scowled at the idea. "No."

"Your favorite word." Julian crossed his arms, biceps clenching as he did. "Why not?"

"Because," she replied and almost left it at that. Julian waited expectantly, smirking smugly as though her lack of reasoning meant he had won. She wasn't about to let him think that. "This isn't about me."

His almond eyes narrowed to slits. "It's a duet. It's about both of us."

"No," she huffed. "As you so obsessively keep pointing out, this dance is for your benefit, to get you into Phoenix. Giving me a solo would only detract the attention away from you."

Julian contemplated her response as he turned to the mirrors and began to stretch. "I'm sure giving you twenty seconds wouldn't do me any harm."

"We don't have time to choreograph any-thing extra." The choreography was finished now and only in need of tweaking. Surely, that was as good an excuse as any.

"We have a month."

"A month to polish this to perfection."

Julian's eyes glittered in the mirror. "You sound like your grandmother."

The words earned an automatic wince from Nora, though she knew he was kidding —

or hoped, anyway. "Why are you pushing this, Julian?"

He shrugged and turned to her again, the smirk wiped from his face now. "I just thought it would work well with what we have. You're a good dancer, Nora. Everybody deserves to see that."

Nora glanced down at the stereo to hide her blush at the compliment. It wasn't that she didn't think she deserved it; it was just that nobody had bothered to praise her dancing before. She had spent her life thinking herself average at best. Having Julian tell her that he noticed her, that he thought she was good... it made her feel bare. It was true she had let herself go these past few weeks, stopped caring so much about what other people must think. Even her grandmother's criticism the other night hadn't made her run the other way, though it had hurt just the same. Maybe she had improved more than she knew.

Finally, she bit down on her lip and met his gaze again. "I don't have anything to prove. I don't need a solo."

Julian sagged with disappointment, and somehow, that felt worse than the idea of dancing alone on the stage. "Alright. If you change your mind—"

"I won't." Nora pulled out her diary and pen, if only to distract herself from his attention, clicking the top incessantly as she perused her schedule. Since she was busier than ever, she had taken the time to copy the schedule Constance had set out for her into a new diary, though she only had the last few months filled in before the new year. "That reminds me," she said aloud, noticing the big block colored in for next weekend. "I can't do next Saturday afternoon. My best friend's getting married."

"No problem." Julian's nonchalance surprised Nora. Usually, he was so uptight about rehearsals, especially as the Winter Showcase drew closer. "Who's the lucky guy?"

Nora's brows knitted together in confusion. "Annie's a lesbian. Weren't you there when they told me they were engaged?"

He scoffed and wiped his feet down before pulling on his socks. It was getting late, and the dark circles around his eyes told her he was exhausted. Good. Maybe he wouldn't force her here before even the birds started singing tomorrow. "I meant, who are you taking as your date?"

"Oh." She shifted, the question taking her aback. He had never paid an interest in her love life before, and in return, she had avoided the subject of Sienna unless they were talking about dance. This felt like crossing a line that Nora wasn't sure she wanted to cross. Then again, hadn't they been dancing on that line all week, with their almost kiss and their very new, very bizarre friendship? "It's not that sort of a wedding, really. It's just a small party in one of the old function rooms we used to dance in as kids. They're getting married at the registry beforehand."

"Not that sort of a wedding?" he repeated suspiciously as he tied his shoelaces. "So there won't be dancing or drinking, then? No fun at all?"

Nora tapped her pen on the table in irritation. "What are you getting at, Julian?"

Julian shrugged his shoulders innocently. "Well, since I just got freed up on Saturday...."

Nora's frown deepened. "You want to come?"

"You're inviting me? Well, sure," he grinned. "Thanks."

Nora rolled her eyes. "Let me rephrase. *Why* do you want to come?"

Julian stood and zipped up his jacket, ruffling his damp hair into a dark tuft of curls. "I just figured if you didn't want to show your face alone, I'd let you drag me along."

"Oh," she sneered, leaning across the table so their faces were inches away. "You'd *let* me? How gracious of you."

His tongue swiped across his bottom lip in amusement. "I'm nothing if not a gentleman. And I can make pretty good arm candy."

The weight of his playful, glittering gaze pressed in on her and she had to straighten and look away. "Not if Annie has a say. She hates your guts. She can join the club."

"You just keep breaking my heart, Cassidy," he complained. "Why does Annie hate me? I barely know her."

"Oh, but she knows you, Julian Walker,"

Nora teased, wiggling her eyebrows as she began to pack up for the day. "She knows you very well."

"She'll know me even better if you invite me to the party."

Nora hesitated and then relented as far as she was willing at the moment. "I'll think about it."

But as soon as she dropped Julian off that night, before falling into the darkness of her own empty apartment, she texted Annie to ask for permission to bring him to the wedding reception. The reply was instant.

As a date?! You have some explaining to do, Nora Cassidy.

And then, a second later:

If you absolutely must bring Julian-effing-Walker to my wedding reception, I suppose you may. Just tell him to behave. I'm not afraid to tear off his balls with my bare hands, and Meg has a black belt in karate.

Nora giggled to herself, face lit only by her phone screen, before typing out her response.

Nothing to explain. Just friends. I'll be sure to tell him that his balls are under threat.

She found Julian's number next, hesitating for only a moment before the keyboard clicked against her fingers.

If you simply cannot spend a Saturday without me, your proposal to join me next weekend has been approved. Just don't be your usual self — Annie has made it very clear that you won't leave the party with your reproductive or-

gans intact if you piss her off.

The bubble of dots popped up immediately as Julian formulated his reply. It took about a minute — not that Nora was fervently watching the time at the top of her screen. Not that her palms were sweating or her fingers shaking slightly.

Still, when the notification finally came, something in her stomach flipped.

I'm terrified for my beloved organs, but for you, Cassidy, I'll risk it. What time am I picking you up?

Nora shook her head as though Julian was still in the room with her, but her mouth ached from the grin curling on her lips.

Just meet me there at seven-ish. This isn't a date.

She sighed and threw her phone on the couch. What on Earth was she doing?

Before she could even contemplate it, her phone lit up again. Another message from Julian sat on her home screen.

If you say so, Cassidy. See you tomorrow.

Twenty-One

Nora's only job for the wedding reception had been hanging the fairy lights, and she had more than fulfilled her duty. The room's wallpaper was peeling and there were questionable stains all over it, but none of that was visible in the dim, golden glow of the lights. She spun around, admiring her work from all angles and ignoring the bartender studying her as though she had lost the plot from behind the counter.

Meg had baked her own wedding cake, it sat in the corner, a classic white, three-tiered work of art with flowers adorning the sides and two brides serving as the cake topper. It was perfect. All of it was perfect.

Tears sprang to Nora's eyes when Annie and Meg walked in, hand in hand, and gasped at the state of the place. Both of them were beautiful: Annie wore tailored gray trousers and a white blouse, while Meg was in a sleek, lacy cocktail dress. They grinned from ear to ear, love softening their gazes as Nora squealed and ran toward them.

"Congratulations! I'm so happy for you." She gathered them both into a tight hug, careful not to accidentally smear her makeup all over their white clothes.

"Thank you," Annie breathed happily. "And thank you for this, Nora. It's so beautiful."

"Of course." Nora pulled away to squeeze their hands, both laden with one new silver band on their fingers. She could feel the happiness brimming from them as if it was her own, warming her bare arms and legs and sending her stomach swooping. They were her family in all of the ways that mattered and she had chosen them as they had chosen her. She was lucky to spend today with them, to celebrate a love Nora did not used to believe could exist. She was glad she had been proven wrong this time.

Their families spilled in behind them, all of them praising the room's decorations. Julian lingered at the back, a head taller than everyone else, which made his discomfort clear as day even from where Nora stood. She cast him a small wave to encourage him over.

Annie whipped her head around and groaned. "I would complain, but I'm too happy," she said. "Just tell me you know what you're doing."

"I know what I'm doing," Nora reassured her with another squeeze of her hand. "We're just friends. Promise."

"Then why is he your date to our wedding?" Meg muttered under her breath, just low enough that Julian couldn't have heard as he reached them. Nora shot her a warning glare.

"Hello," Julian greeted, holding out his hand and shaking first Annie's and then Meg's hand. In his other, he held an expensive bottle of red wine that Nora knew neither of them would enjoy. Still, it was the thought that counted. "Congratulations to you both. It's all downhill from here, they say."

Nora practically choked on his aftershave as he took his place beside her, his hand finding her waist as though clinging onto the one person who could tolerate him for dear life. Still, she sank into him without really thinking about it, used to his touch. Surprisingly, he had made quite the effort. His muscles rippled beneath his navy blue shirt and black tailored trousers, even his hair was slightly more styled than usual and tucked away from his face.

That did nothing to help his terrible joke, though, and Meg and Annie both blinked warily. "We'd better go and greet our guests," Meg suggested.

Annie agreed fervently and the two of them wandered off to their family, but not before Meg mimicked a karate chop behind Julian's back. Nora had to stifle a giggle. Julian blew out a harsh breath in their absence.

Nora frowned. "I know I said not to act your usual self, but what was that?"

"I have no idea," he grimaced. And then, as though it was the first time he had really seen her, his eyes lingered on her — first her face, painted with more makeup than she usually bothered with, and falling down to the low-cut chiffon dress she had bought earlier this week. It fell to her knees, but despite the cold, she hadn't bothered with tights — a mistake, she realized, as she surveyed them herself and saw they were peppered with friction burns and bruises from rehearsals. "You clean up well, Cassidy."

She rolled her eyes and tried not to let the compliment affect her, though it did. She was beginning to tingle with it, actually. "Not so bad yourself, Walker."

She took the wine from him and placed it on the gifts table. When her only means of distraction was gone, she worried at her lip. "So."

"So," he echoed, mouth twitching at the corners. God, she hated how good he looked when he did that, his cheeks dimpling and his brown eyes turning to soft caramel. "Can I buy you a drink?"

"No need. Open bar," Nora beamed.

Julian's grin widened as he took her hand. "Even better."

Nora was glowing, and it was making it hard for Julian to think of anything else. He downed three highball glasses of rum and Coke, but it only bolstered the fire that had been crackling in his belly for weeks. He wanted to run his hands through her red gold hair, wanted to hold her hand forever. It had been difficult to ignore when they were dancing. Now, it was impossible.

When she left to talk to the other guests, he could only watch her and the way her dress twirled with every movement, golden sunlight seemed to pour out of her smile, her pale skin caught the moonlight dripping in from the window and kept it for itself. More than that, though, he didn't want to make a fool of himself any more than he already had in front of her friends. He wanted them to like him.

It was not something he'd ever cared about before.

They watched the first dance and the cutting of the cake side by side. She never strayed from him for too long, as though she could feel him pulling her back with just his eyes. She didn't want him to think she'd forgotten him.

They laughed together with complete ease and cut into the line when the buffet opened without even feeling bad about it. She put a profiterole on his plate because he had never tried one before, and in return, he let her have all of his ice cream.

It was so easy. Why hadn't it always been this easy?

The music slowed as the night wore on, and while Nora was ordering more drinks at the bar, Julian stopped her before she could pick them up and held out his hand. "It wouldn't be right not to dance at a wedding."

Nora raised an eyebrow hesitantly. "I don't know. Do we want to put everyone else to show?"

"If you think my answer to that would ever be 'no,' you don't know me at all."

A breathy laugh escaped as she put her hand in his. "You're right. Arrogant bastard." Her tone, for once, was all teasing, and he laughed with her as he pulled her onto the floor. The fairy lights danced above them as they began to sway. Nora looked down as he placed her hands around his neck. They only just reached, and that was because she wore heels tonight. Her eyelashes caught the shadows and sent them running across her glittering cheekbones.

"Why did you want to come tonight, Julian?"

"Because I love being a constant annoyance in your life," he taunted, hands sliding to meet at her spine. She was warm and soft in his hands, and though he had held her like this in rehearsals a million times before, everything felt different now. "And soon, I won't be able to be."

"You'll have to find someone else." She feigned disgust. The smell of sweet wine clung to her breath, her eyes swam with it. She wasn't drunk yet, but she might have been had he not stopped her from ordering their last round. "Someone who isn't nearly as witty with their comebacks. How will you manage?"

"I won't." It was true. He had spent every waking moment with her these last couple of months. It would be a stark shock to go without her now, to dance with somebody else who didn't know him the way she did, who couldn't anticipate his next move or choreograph with his style in mind. "There's only one Nora Cassidy."

"And thank heavens for that," she replied dryly.

He dipped her as the chorus came, admiring the golden column of her neck as she arched back up, breasts pressing against his torso and hips hard against his. She spun without needing him to guide her, twirling beneath his arm before stumbling and clutching onto him again as she laughed at her own clumsiness.

That laugh. That laugh could turn him into ashes and dust and he'd still want to hear it again. It wasn't light or tinkling; it was hearty and tumbled straight from her belly until it was louder than the music playing. He could do nothing but laugh with her.

He lifted her gently, reveling in every moment of contact as she slid back down his body and clung onto him like a tidal wave to a rock in a tempest.

He had been grossly downplaying how she looked earlier. She didn't just clean up well; she was an angel in corporeal form tonight in her emerald dress, her copper hair spilling onto her shoulders. He ran a finger through it carefully, brushing it off her face. Her eyes fluttered when his knuckle grazed her cheek.

"Why are you really here, Julian?" She was practically begging him with that whisper. He couldn't deny her.

"Because…" He sighed in an attempt to find the right words. "Because I like being around you. I want to be around you always, and soon, I might not be able to see you, and I think that might make me miserable."

Her breath hitched in surprise as he pulled her closer, bowing his head as she consumed him completely.

"You have no idea what you do to me, Cassidy," he murmured, tilting her chin up gently.

Her eyes gleamed as she returned his gaze unwaveringly. "No. I don't think I do."

He swallowed. He could so easily kiss her, but if he did, it could ruin him just as much as it could save him. He needed her — as a friend, a dance partner, the woman who stuck up for him and his brother in front of his father, and the woman who cheered for him when his audition went well. She hadn't given up on him once, even when he had deserved it. If something happened, if they ruined this now….

"Are you going to keep staring at me or are you going to kiss me?" she asked impatiently.

A chuckle rumbled out of him, soon stolen by her lips. He could barely breathe through it. The music, lights, even the other guests disappeared. All that existed was her and perhaps him, though with the way his knees wobbled and his chest soared, he couldn't even be certain of that.

"I want to take you home," he muttered against her lips when they came up for air.

"Pervert," she whispered, breath ragged. Just when he thought he'd ruined it by being too forward, her mouth grazed his again — teasing. She was teasing him. She knew exactly what she was doing now and she was relishing in her new-found power. Even in his state, with his heart beating fiercely and his stomach searing with desire, the familiar irritation that pulsed through him for only her returned.

"Nora," he begged like a child through gritted teeth.

He could taste her grin when they locked together a final time. "You'd better call a cab then."

Twenty-Two

Nora didn't know which was more surprising: that Julian Walker was kissing her or that she was letting him. She let him over and over again in the cab ride home and up the stairs, and those kisses turned hungry when she finally unlocked the door and they stumbled into the apartment together.

"What are we doing?" she asked as they fell into the bedroom, his mouth roving her neck, the crook of her shoulder, her collarbone. Her hands tangled in his hair, goosebumps rising on her skin. Everything between them was electric, their skin made of static. She could feel it jolting between them. "Do you do this with all of your dance partners?"

It was a joke, but a part of her did wonder. His last relationship was Sienna. Blonde, perfect, prima ballerina Sienna. They were polar opposites, with only one thing in common. Him. Was this just what he did? Did this mean nothing?

"Not intentionally." His breath was cool against her hot skin as his fingers found the zipper of her dress, right between her shoulder blades. She shivered. "Do you still want this?"

She didn't know what mangled plea would

come out if she opened her mouth, so instead she only nodded. The way his fingers brushed her jaw took her by surprise. She had half expected him to rip the chiffon off and have his way with her. Instead, he moved delicately, locking eyes with her for a moment before he kissed her hair, her ear-lobe, until his fingers finally crept back to the zip-per. She unraveled with the dress when he freed her from it, the material spilling by her feet so that she was laid bare, save for her underwear.

He drank her in painstakingly slowly, his gaze roaming every inch of her skin as though he could touch her with just those blazing eyes. In an-other life, she would have been self-conscious, but not that night. Not with him. Still, instinct left her frozen — waiting, perhaps, for him to say he had made a mistake.

He didn't. Instead, the single word, "beau-tiful," fell from his lips in a labored gasp, fringed with awe and desire.

Nora's chest heaved as she found the but-tons of his shirt and undid them one by one, en-joying the way he waited patiently, hungrily. She had never felt wanted like this before. It didn't make her want to cover up and run away. It made her want to give him every shard of her she could stand to lose. All of the parts of herself she had kept protected all this time, they would be his now. To break or to cherish, she didn't care.

"Nora." That plea almost sent her to her knees. Before she could undo the last button, his fingers were in her hair, his lips pressing against hers desperately. When his hands slid beneath her thighs and she wrapped her legs around his waist, she felt as though she was dancing with him still, she was no longer afraid to trust him as he lowered her onto the bed with measured control, as though he could keep her suspended in the shadowy space between for hours.

She did not have the same restraint. As soon as she met the mattress, she weaved herself into him and around him, her hands sweeping down his chest and her heels scraping the back of his thighs. When he groaned, she kicked them off, and they landed with a thud on the carpet. The fire she felt when she danced with him had turned into a spitting inferno now, wracking her entire body with flames that centred in the apex of her thighs.

She wanted him. All of him. No more dancing around it.

As though sensing it, Julian kissed her with frenzied force, his hands exploring her rocky vertebrae, the curve of her hips, her waist. His fingers curled into the soft flesh there as though asking her permission. She granted it by bunching up his shirt, helping him to finally slide it off.

And then, at the sight of his bare skin and toned abdomen, she realized what exactly she had given him permission to do. What it meant. She froze with her hands still on his chest, his legs still bracketed by hers. He leaned in to kiss her again. She couldn't let him.

His eyes lightened as he pulled away from her and tucked her untamed hair behind her ear. She wished he hadn't; she liked the protection it gave her when it fell around her face like a veil. "We don't have to do this," he offered. "We can stop."

"Do you want to?" she asked, feeling timid all of a sudden. All that remained between them was her underwear and his trousers. If they took these final steps, those would be gone, too, and there would be nothing left to keep them apart.

He shook his head, and she could tell by the way his golden eyes glistened that he meant it. "Only if you do."

"I don't want to mess things up. We're so close to the showcase, Julian." The vulnerability made her croak.

"I know." His face was shrouded by shadows, and only then did she realize that she hadn't even turned the light on when they got in. She flicked on her bedside lamp now, twisting away from him for only an instant — but it was an instant too long. She wanted this. She wanted him.

His calloused hands cradled her face. "Why can't we just be what we are and figure the rest out after the show? No complications. No distractions."

"You think we can?"

"I think that I've wanted this — *you* — for a while, and if you feel the same... I don't want to waste tonight." She swallowed nervously against his words. "Just tell me what you want, Nora. Tell me to leave, and I'll leave."

She couldn't tell him that. She didn't want to be left cold again. "Don't leave," she said. "Stay."

She reached for the button of his trousers and he stepped out of them quickly before returning to the space between her legs. He found the clasp of her bra and unfastened it with ease, letting her breasts spill out. She didn't want to hide from him anymore, so she didn't. She let him wander her body like a traveler, let him leave traces of himself across every nook and swell as her firsts curled into the bedsheets desperately.

They rose and fell together as though their bodies still thought they were in the studio. When it came to it, he knew exactly where to clutch the dips of her waist to have her squirming. He knew that the vulnerable, silver-striped spots of her inner thighs longed for his mouth. In return, she knew to drag her delicate fingers down the lines of his stomach until she reached the waistband of his boxers and felt him shudder and harden beneath her. She knew that when her breath grazed his earlobe, his eyes would flutter shut.

Her body knew his — had for weeks, months — and his knew hers. When he finally brushed first his fingers and then his lips against the sensitive spot between her thighs before giving himself to her completely, her back rising from the mattress with the overwhelming pleasure of them finally slotting together, it did not feel wrong or

messy. It felt as it always had with him.
It felt like dancing.

Twenty-Three

Julian awoke to sunlight made human. Nora's hair spilled across the pillows beside him, dripping liquid copper onto the silk covers. The pale, delicate fingers that had buried themselves so aggressively into his back last night were splayed and twitching in dream. Julian could make out every green, curling vein and every dark blemish beneath her translucent skin, and he wanted to kiss every inch of her all over again, but he didn't want to wake her yet. Let her have this peace. Let them both have it. It had been a long time coming, with their constant wars.

As he brushed her hair away to find her face, carved into a glorious mask of tranquillity, he prayed that those wars were a thing of the past. They would always bicker, of course. She was stubborn as a mule, and he could be a pain in the ass when he wanted to be, but he could live with that. Would relish it, in fact. He would rather quarrel with her than laugh with anyone else in the world. Better still if they could keep this bliss that came in between, when they were sleeping beside each other or dancing with the same heartbeats.

He had never been more certain of what he

wanted, because it was lying in front of him. He still tingled with it, could still taste her whimpers of pleasure on his lips. Last night, she had curled herself around him so completely, had made a home in the crater beneath his rib cage. He had not even noticed until then just how deep her roots had buried themselves in him. God help him if they were ever unearthed.

She stirred, nestling herself into his chest as though she sought him even before unconsciousness had cleared. He smiled to himself, savoring the last of this stillness with her, and pulled her closer, his palm pressed against the soft skin of her stomach. He couldn't remember the last time he had felt needed, wanted, like this — if he ever had.

Then, her mouth gaped open as she groaned out a mangled yawn and her body stiffened in a stretch and it was shattered. Her eyes fluttered open slowly, still heavy with the makeup she hadn't had the chance to clean off last night. She squinted into the morning light before settling her bewildered gaze on him.

"Morning, Cassidy," he murmured, planting a soft kiss in her hairline. He dreaded to think that it might have been the last time she would let him. It wasn't as though he deserved her, after all he had done. "You snore like my grandad."

"Well, you kick in your sleep, karate kid," she shot back, still quick as a whip to put him in his place even half asleep. It warmed him, igniting him into flames all over again.

"You must piss me off even when I'm dreaming," he smirked. "Probably a sign I shouldn't be in your bed." It was a weak joke he instantly regretted. Any moment, her eyes could turn back to that frosty green and he could be shoved back out of her bed, out of her life.

They didn't, though. Instead, she blinked the sleep out of her eyes before looking up at him and smiling crookedly. "And yet here you are."

"Here I am." His toes curled as he stretched, breath catching in his throat, and then he let his hands dance across her bare shoulders and tangle into her hair. He kissed her lazily, and she let him, her legs twisting their way through the bedsheets until they locked with his. Last night's heat was not gone, but with the peace he felt lying here, it had simmered into a dull ache that he was sure would flare again later, when they were practicing and his hands were on her hips, her thighs, her spine. The thought made him shiver.

"Ugh," she grimaced, hands pushing against his bare chest. "Morning stubble."

Julian laughed and ran his hands over the rough bristles on his chin. "You're one to talk, with all the scratches you left on me last night."

She pouted like a child and he realized that her lips were still swollen with his kisses. He tried not to let that knowledge reach the place where his lust dwelled quietly. To distract himself, he shimmied on his boxers beneath the duvet before crawling painfully out of bed. "Breakfast?"

Nora whined as though his absence left her aching and began to scramble for her own clothes. "Coffee first."

"Coffee." He made a show of gagging as he flicked on the kettle. "Disgusting."

He browsed the cupboards until he found a set of mugs, but as he closed the door, a picture hanging on the wall caused him to falter. It was a braces-wearing, preteen Nora, beaming beside her dad outside the dance studio. He had never seen her eyes glitter the way they did behind the frame's glass. Her father's adoration was clear on his face, too; they shared the same deep-set dimples that bracketed their grins, and their doe eyes wrinkled identically in the corners.

Julian was vaguely aware of the sound of Nora's bare feet padding against the floor until she stopped beside him to gauge what had left him frozen. He swallowed down his regret, his sorrow for that little girl. She didn't need it. She had become strong and wonderful all on her own.

He turned to find her wearing nothing but an oversized shirt, the sleeves rolled up haphazardly. Her hair was ruffled into a nest at the back, where she had lain on the pillow. The sight made him soften as he placed the mugs down on the counter. The kettle grumbled to a stop, but he couldn't move enough yet to pour the water.

"Oh," she let out in strained realization finally.

"You both look so happy there," he said.

"We were." She averted her attention to a splinter of chipped wood on the edge of the counter. "He would have been so disappointed if he knew I'd walked away from it all. He loved dance. He wanted me to love dance."

"And you do," he argued, grazing her hands with his knuckles before weaving their fingers together. "You're here, aren't you?"

"Because, between you and Constance, I was practically forced against my will."

"Because you cared enough to come back, even after everything. If the studio didn't matter to you, you would have left it in the dust years ago. Just because you stopped dancing in front of people doesn't mean you stopped dancing altogether. Your father would know that."

She sighed shakily and pulled out two tea bags, dropping them in the mugs. Julian didn't deign to remind her that she had requested coffee. "Maybe."

"He would have been proud of you no matter what. How could he not be?"

A small, appreciative smile graced her lips as she picked up the kettle. He pulled it away from her to pour it himself — couldn't she just let him do something for her for once? — and she crouched to pull the milk from the fridge.

"Use it sparingly," she ordered as she handed it to him.

"I know how to make a good cup of tea, thank you very much," he chided in response, putting no more than a drop of milk in each mug before twisting the lid back on. For once, her brows raised in approval.

"Does it bother you that Sienna left?" Nora questioned into the fridge as she put the milk back, as though she had been waiting to ask and thought it better to avoid his gaze when she finally did.

He only had to take a moment to ponder before he replied. "It did for a while. Now I'm glad."

"You're glad?" Nora repeated in disbelief. "Weren't you together for years?"

"Out of convenience, mostly," he explained, sliding the mug over to her and leaning against the counter. He had to be careful not to bang his head against the corner of the cupboards.

"Still, she abandoned you when you needed her help most."

"And if she hadn't, I wouldn't have got this," he admitted quietly, warming his hands against the steaming mug of tea. The bitter, earthy smell roused him from his sleepiness, made him realize this wasn't a dream. Nora was here, in nothing but an old shirt, and he had... well, he had made love to her last night.

It had never been like that before. He had had enough sex to know that it was so much more than that with Nora, so much more intense. To see her that way, trusting him, letting him caress every inch of her without fear... it had made him come undone in a way he never had before.

"You," he elaborated finally, sipping the tea

and scalding his tongue in the process. "I wasn't in love with Sienna." *I'm in love with you.* The words remained unsaid, but he was just as certain of them as he was that she had heard them escape beneath the silence.

He wasn't sure when he had danced across that line between hate and love. The previous night had cemented it, yes, but it had been festering in him for a while now. Perhaps it had always been there somewhere, bubbling beneath the arguments. Nobody had ever made him feel — whether that feeling was burning hate, love, lust, awe, or all that came in between — more than she did.

When she gazed at him, he couldn't be sure whether it was requited. The air was stiff with all that remained unsaid, and he couldn't move, couldn't breathe until Nora's phone buzzed on the bedside table and she snapped away to get it. Her brows knitted together as she tucked her mussed hair behind her ear and scanned the screen.

"Everything okay?"

"I have a text from Constance," Nora muttered distantly. "She never texts me."

"Do I dare ask what she wants?"

"She wants me to meet her for lunch." Her frown deepened as she looked up. "At her house. God, I haven't been there since I moved out."

Julian didn't like the way her voice shook. He placed his mug down, lips pressed into a thin line. "I can come with you if you want. I'm not much of a mediator, but I'll try to keep my mouth shut."

"No." She threw her phone on the bed and looked around the apartment as though she was lost. Her dress was still inside out on the floor, her bra not too far from it, and her heels in two separate corners. His own shirt was crumpled in a heap with his trousers. With the weight of what they had done, the passion that had accompanied it, Julian was surprised the whole apartment hadn't crumbled. "No, I'll be okay."

Nora pulled a sweater and leggings from her closet and began to slide them on. Flashes of milky skin reminded Julian of last night and his face prickled with searing heat. He wanted her again. Wanted her always.

He forced his eyes to his tea. "You sure?"

"I won't subject you to my grandmother any more than you need to be," she said breathlessly. "You can stay here as long as you like. The keys are in the door. Make sure you lock up when you leave."

"I was going to leave the door wide open and let the burglars have their way," he replied sarcastically behind his mug, glancing at the clock on the wall. "Are you going now?"

"Have you ever kept Constance Cassidy waiting?" She combed through her hair in the mirror and used the pad of her finger to wipe away her smeared mascara.

"No," Julian quipped, "but I've kept Nora Cassidy waiting and I can imagine the terrifying similarities. What about rehearsal?"

"I'll come to the studio when I'm done." As though remembering, Nora threw a sports bra and vest top into her bag for later and slid on her sneakers.

Julian feigned hurt and tutted. "I can't believe you're running out on me. I'm surprised you didn't sneak out at dawn, heartbreaker."

"Oh, shut up." Nora rolled her eyes and ambled over to him, her arms curling around him and her fingers digging into the nape of his neck, where night-old sweat still clung to his hair. He breathed her in, placing down his mug so he could clutch her waist. "Last night was…."

"I know," he agreed, saving her the effort of finding words. None would be enough for what last night was. He ached with the memory.

"We'll talk about it later?"

"We will. Now, are you going to kiss me again, Cassidy, or are you going to leave a man waiting forever?"

The corner of her mouth curled into a smile and then she was all over him again, her tongue running across the seam of his lips. He felt her melt into him, and if not for the counter holding him up, they might have collapsed altogether. "Are you sure we don't have time—"

"No," she whispered, eyes fluttering shut as he placed a final peck on the tip of her upturned nose. Her hands roamed his bare chest, not daring to go any lower. She knew by now what that did to him. "Later."

"I'll keep you to that promise." Julian suppressed a groan when she pulled away. "Good luck."

"Thanks," she sighed, tying her hair into a ponytail before heading to the door. "I'll need it."

A smile danced on Julian's lips as he flashed her a small wave and she returned it. Their eyes lingered across the room long enough that he forgot where he was, and then she was gone.

Her ghost still followed him across the apartment, though, her perfume clinging to the bedsheets and her photographs watching him along the walls. He basked in those small dregs of her until it was time to leave.

Twenty-Four

Constance's house was so big that Nora couldn't find her in it. She rang the doorbell and received no answer, but the door had been unlocked, so she had searched high and low, through marbled hallways and the pristine kitchen. On her way to the study, she had stumbled past her old childhood room and she couldn't help herself. She slid inside quietly, as though she was a thief in the night, afraid of being caught.

She didn't know why, not when she stepped in and closed the door. Why had she felt the need to see it again? To remember? To wrap herself up in the bitter nostalgia of less pleasant times? This had been the home of a sad little girl who had lost the only family who cared for her. Her grief was written all over these white walls, plastered over with polka dot wallpaper and the old, tarnished posters of dancers she had put up despite Constance's disapproval. They were her father's. Much of this room belonged to him: his old, knitted blanket, still folded neatly on the edge of the bed; the paintings leaning against the wall; the hoodies Nora had waited and waited to grow into and now couldn't bring herself to wear. It had been too painful to take it all with her, so she had left it here. Constance had never asked her to clear it out.

Though it was untouched, no dust sprinkled the room. Nora ran her finger over the dresser to be sure, but it came away clean. Perhaps Constance had forgotten to tell her maids that there was no use in cleaning it... but in four years? It seemed unlikely.

She was glad to find that the room no longer felt like hers, that she recalled all of the lonely nights spent tangled in the silk sheets of that bed with distant indistinction. No feelings accompanied them other than a vague sadness for the girl she had once been but was not anymore. She had moved on. Grown up. Freed herself as much as she could bear without losing dance altogether. Maybe Julian had been right this morning. Maybe her father would have been proud regardless.

"Do you feel old?"

The voice came from behind her. Nora started and turned, finding Constance in the doorway. She flashed Nora a watery smile as she stepped in and closed the door.

"I couldn't find you," Nora explained guiltily, drawing away from the dresser.

"I was getting dressed."

At midday? Nora wondered but didn't dare question. "Oh," was all she could breathe out.

Constance glanced around wistfully, her eyes a cloudy gray. She was all skin and bone these days — not that she had ever been much else when she was younger. Still, her cheeks had hollowed recently, her walk grown unsteady. It was confusing to see her as an old, frail lady. Nora had never thought it possible — had half expected she'd never age at all. "How is the routine going with Mr. Walker?"

Nora frowned. Was she making small talk? Even the idea was ridiculous. "Well," Nora responded politely, wringing her hands together. "It's going well."

Constance nodded knowingly. "You seem to have put your differences aside, anyhow. That man cares deeply for you."

Nora turned to hide her blush, fiddling with an old music box. A ballerina remained frozen in arabesque in the center. She had long since lost her life, her ability to sing and twirl. "What makes you say that?"

"He made it very clear when he barged into my office and made his distaste for my..." she searched for the words before settling on, "constructive criticism known. He's like a little lap dog, that one. His bark is worse than his bite."

Nora could say nothing. She had suspected that Julian had said something to Constance when she left that night, since it had taken a while for him to come out after her, but she couldn't have predicted he would have stood up for her... protected her, even. "I didn't know he did that."

"He must fancy himself a silent hero, then." Constance forced out a tight-lipped smile.

"Why am I here, Constance?" Nora burst out before she could be distracted. "You never invite me here."

"You never wish to come when I do."

"Does that surprise you?" It was an effort for Nora to keep her voice steady and low. Being here, in her old room, in her old house, magnified all of the hurt and anger she had felt toward Constance this past decade or so and brought all of the things she should have said as a teenager, when it might have been excused as hormones and mood swings, up from the depths where she had long ago buried them. She had always kept her mouth shut and stayed clear as best she could, which wasn't difficult when it was only the two of them rattling around the place. She dreaded to think how quiet it must be with only Constance here, alone with all this space. No wonder she had practically lived at the studio until recently.

"Let us have this conversation at the dining table, shall we?"

"No," she found herself saying bluntly. "Whatever this is, whatever bribe or blackmail or criticism you've thought up this time, let's hear it now. I won't be torn down again while you mimic courteousness."

"Stubborn as muck, just like your father," Constance sighed, as though to herself. "Very well. I wished to talk to you about my reasons for retiring. As my granddaughter, I thought you had the right to know."

"I'm not your granddaughter." Nora shook her head in disbelief. "I'm a lot of things, Constance — your student, your subject of abuse, your way of feeling superior when you belittle me — but I haven't been your granddaughter in a very long time. You've made that clear. I—"

"I'm unwell, Nora," Constance interrupted, voice brittle. "Dying, perhaps."

The air turned to ice. Nora's mouth fell open and then shut and then open again, her stomach swirling with confusion, fear, dread, sadness, regret, and guilt, though she had every right to feel nothing at all. The words didn't make sense. Constance was not the sort of woman to fall ill, and she certainly wasn't the sort of woman to show that weakness to Nora.

It was pathetic, but Nora could only whisper a flat "Oh."

"That's what they tell me, anyway," Constance continued, chin still held high — though Nora spotted the slight wobble to it. "I feel fit as a fiddle, really. However, facing the possibility of the end… it is cruel. It makes you very aware of all the ways in which you've failed. I have been too cold and too proud. Your father would have despised the way I raised you. He always did wish I was more loving, to both him and you. You're right. I was no grandmother."

Nora couldn't find the words to agree or disagree. Her mind had emptied, its contents replaced with a black void that provided her no respite or response.

Constance, to Nora's surprise, laughed feebly. "I always thought they would pull my rotting corpse from the studio, but I've been receiving treatment, you see. It hasn't been working so well." Nora's heart thundered in her chest. She collapsed into the foamy mattress in shock. "It means I will have to continue with something much stronger. I won't be fit to run the studio for much longer. I won't be fit for much at all. I have no choice but to surrender it to you."

The word "surrender" echoed in Nora's mind, as though this was a battle that Constance had already lost. As though giving the studio to Nora was a last resort.

"Is it terminal?"

"There's hope for me yet, apparently," Constance smirked dryly. "But I'm not getting any younger, child. There's a possibility I won't recover."

And then what? Constance was a terrible excuse for a family, but she was all that Nora had left. Her mother had walked away before Nora had even the time to memorize her face, and her father was not coming back. Everything she had been tied to from birth remained in this house, in this room. What would happen when it left?

She swallowed down the questions, knowing they would only make her seem silly. It was too late to show that she cared. "Thank you for telling me."

Constance nodded and reached out. Nora watched her bony hand wearily as it fell to her cheek and then remained still, as though Constance didn't know what to do with it next. Her palm was cold and disconcerting. "I am sorry, Nora. I did fail you. I know that better than anyone."

Nora's eyes filled with tears, they were caught in Constance's hand.

"But I am glad you are dancing again. You bring light to that studio — the best trait you could have inherited from your father. I saw what you did for that boy, Julian's brother. I once wished that you were more like me, but now, I thank the heavens that you're not. I see none of my cruelty and all of your father's love. I have nothing but faith that you will do as he wished and make that place beautiful again."

Nora bit down on her trembling lip and looked to the picture of her father, stuck beneath the mirror's frame. It was the only one she had left here because it was the last one taken of him before the accident, and it hurt too much to see every day, but suddenly, it was a comfort. She wanted what Constance wanted. She wanted to be like him and make the studio beautiful, accepting, and free of the resentment and dread she had felt growing up there. She wanted to make him proud, and she finally had the chance.

"The studio is yours, Nora," Constance breathed. "You have proven worthy already."

Constance's hand fell into Nora's and squeezed. Nora squeezed back timidly, feeling for the first time what it would have been like to have a grandmother growing up rather than just a dance teacher whose house she happened to live in.

"You can trust me with the studio. I'll do my best with it," Nora vowed. "I'll make my father proud."

A smile Nora had never seen before creased Constance's face into a myriad of lines. "You already have. I'm certain of that, my dear."

Twenty-Five

Julian had been awaiting Nora in the studio for over an hour, his hands trembling with the anticipation of seeing her again. Nothing had changed. Everything had changed. His heart had been hammering against his rib cage all day because of it.

But when she finally did make her appearance, she did not seem quite as eager to see him and his stomach sunk. She walked in wearing an indecipherable expression and slid her shoes off without even untying her laces. Anger bubbled immediately in Julian. *What had Constance said to her now? What had she done?*

"Is everything alright?"

"Fine," she answered blankly.

Julian frowned and made his way over to her. He was already slick with sweat, dust clung to the soles of his feet after having practiced alone. "What did she say?"

"Nothing important," Nora replied, rolling up the sleeves of her sweater. Her absent gaze, which shifted everywhere but onto him, caused a pang of panic to shoot through him. Maybe this wasn't about Constance. Maybe she regretted last night once she had time to think about it. "Let's get on with it, shall we?"

"I thought we could talk first."

"About what?"

Julian's eyes narrowed. Was she trying to hurt him? Had this all been part of some plan to get back at him? Maybe she had never stopped hating him. Maybe she didn't care at all. "About last night. About us."

"We don't have time for that." Nora drew the curtain across the floor, the silk picking up grime. She still hadn't looked at him, but he saw under the lights that she was pale, her lips pursed with tension.

"I don't understand." He fought to keep his voice from wavering as he followed her, gripping the curtain so her attention would be forced away from it. "You left your apartment smiling from ear to ear this morning."

"Someone thinks a lot of himself," she muttered as she huffed out a breath. There was none of her usual smirking or teasing, though. The words were flat, meaningless.

"Now you won't even look at me," he continued as though he hadn't heard her. Dread dripped into his stomach and into his words, pooling into a puddle of ice in the very pits of him. "How could you have changed your mind that quickly?"

"You said we'd figure things out after the show," she accused. "So let's do that. No distractions, right?"

"Right." He clenched his jaw as the ice flooded through him now. "So we're just going back to this?"

"To what?"

"This," he motioned to something invisible in front of them. "Fighting. Constantly at one another's throats."

"We're not going back to anything. Are we rehearsing or not?" When her eyes finally locked on his, he wished they hadn't. They were as glazed as green glass, like a wine bottle floating in the middle of the freezing cold sea while a storm raged. The weight of them, the edge of them, made him want to sink away into nothing. It was everything he had woken up and feared this morning. Did she have any idea what it did to him?

She couldn't have. Nora was a lot of things, but cruel was not one of them. Even in their most personal arguments, she had never crossed a line with him, never given him any more than a faint bruise to his ego. This, here, was not a faint bruise. This was an open wound, and he was bleeding all over the floor in front of her.

He stepped away and patched himself up, composing himself. If she wanted to play like this again, he wouldn't be the weak one. He wouldn't beg.

"Get the music, then." A bitter scowl twisted onto his lips as he got into position behind the curtain. She did as asked, plugging her phone into the stereo and playing the music before rushing back into the center of the floor to meet him.

They danced as they always did and as they never had before, not because they were doing it well but because Nora was somewhere he could not reach. They were two castes of marble brushing into one another without ever touching. They did not share their usual glances when she landed across him on the floor or when he lifted her and she slid down his body as she had at the wedding. They were strangers who happened to be dancing to the same music. It was as though everything, all those hours of practice and laughing and fighting, had been erased. There was not even hatred to fall back on.

There was nothing. Nothing at all.
And it killed him.

∞∞∞

Nora could have told him if she'd wanted to. She had walked into the studio half expecting she would crumble at the sight of him and blurt out everything that had just happened with Constance. Instead, she found herself cold and closed off, just as she had been after her father had died. Just as Constance always was.

It was a coping mechanism she couldn't disable, no matter how often she noticed Julian flinching away from her as they practiced. They barely said more than a few words after almost an hour of being at it. They had thrown themselves into the dance to avoid conversation, but she couldn't focus on the movements anymore, and her feet were clumsy, numb stubs at the end of her legs that kept stumbling over the steps.

And then, when Julian placed Nora down from a lift and they fell into their next step, their legs entangled with the curtain. She could feel herself falling and see him falling from the corner of her eye, too. She tried to grab onto him or the silk or anything at all, but his foot twisted beneath hers, and then they were both on the floor with a loud thud. The music still played, but the panic drowned out the melody. All Nora could hear was her own heartbeat thundering in her ears and Julian cursing with labored gasps.

She pulled herself up slowly. She had landed on her wrist, which was throbbing ominously, but she had been injured enough times to know it would only take an ice pack or two and perhaps a bandage to heal. Julian, though....

He was nursing his ankle in a sitting position, his face a sickly, pallid shade that highlighted the deep circles under his eyes. "Fuck. Fuck. Shit."

"Julian—"

"What the fuck have you done, Nora?" His words were strained with pain and panic. She had never seen him like this: terrified. His hair was in his eyes, his entire body was taught as he clutched his ankle desperately. "My fucking ankle...."

"Oh, god. I'm so sorry," she cried desperately, sliding across the floor to meet him and see the damage. "I tripped."

"No shit," he barked in contempt.

She fussed over him with trembling hands, but when her skin grazed his, he stiffened. "Don't touch me."

"Julian, please, let me look," she pleaded. One of them was going to break. Any moment, one of them would shatter, and she couldn't be sure if it would be her from the guilt or him from the anger and pain.

"You've done enough," he spat out. His entire body shook and he guarded his ankle from her with his arms protectively.

"Can you move it?"

He did, rotating it half an inch before he flinched in agony. "Fuck. I think it's sprained."

Dread gnawed at Nora. A sprain, weeks before the showcase. It could ruin everything.

"We should get you to the hospital." She tried to reach for him again but he drew away before she could get close.

"Do you have any idea what this could do to me, Nora?" His eyes glittered with tears. She wanted to apologize, to fix this, but she couldn't. She couldn't do anything but look at him and beg silently for forgiveness. If he would just calm down, they could work through this, go to the hospital and figure out a plan. "Do you have any fucking idea?"

"It was an accident," she whispered, suppressing a sob. "I'm sorry, Julian. I'm so, so sorry."

"Are you?" Cruelty and accusation distorted his features. "Or is this payback for what I did to you at the competition?"

Nora's face wrinkled in bewilderment. "What?"

"It's perfect, really, isn't it?" he sneered. "I drop you on stage and it ruins your life, so you wait until I need you most — need *this* most — to get me back."

"Do you honestly think I'm capable of that?" Defensively, she sat back on her hands and thrust herself up despite the twinge in her wrist. "Do you honestly believe I could do that to you, Julian?"

"It's awfully convenient." His throat bobbed as he pulled himself up, too. She didn't try to help him, not even when he staggered and hopped, keeping the weight off his right foot. His best foot, she knew. "You hated me with a passion for years."

Nora shook her head in disbelief. She could say nothing. *Do* nothing. Her guilt was replaced by hurt. After everything, he thought she could be *that* spiteful? He didn't know her at all. He had never known her. And she had never known him.

He didn't wait for a response, instead picking up his shoes by the mirror and limping slowly to the door. His t-shirt clung to his back from sweat, the muscles rolling in his shoulders from the effort it took just to walk.

She slid her own sneakers on and followed

him out quickly, scrambling through her purse for her car keys. Apparently, he was wise enough to know he couldn't drive in his state because he stopped by her car instead of his own and waited for her to open it. She did, numbly, waiting until he had slid into the passenger side before she got in.

They said nothing for the whole ride. When they reached the hospital, Nora signed him in at the front desk while he took a seat. Everything felt a million miles away: the fluorescent lights, the nurses brushing past her in pale blue scrubs, the smell of disinfectant. It was strangely quiet for the ER, but she didn't question it, instead pulling at the loose threads of her sweater while she waited beside him wordlessly.

When the doctor came out to call Julian's name, she didn't follow him into the ward, and he didn't ask her to. She sat there, as she had been already, and stared at the same three gray stripes on the wall. A television blared in the corner. She didn't hear it. Ambulance sirens wailed outside, but they sounded to her more like a distant hum. The day's date was scrawled in black pen on the whiteboard in front of her. The same date it had been this morning.

This morning, when she had woken happy in his arms.

That was all broken now. That was all gone.

It occurred to her then that this was the hospital where she had said goodbye to her father and also where she had been rushed after falling off the stage at the competition five years ago. It was probably the same hospital Constance would come to soon, too.

It seemed as though this was the place where Nora lost things… lost everything, perhaps.

And all she could do was sit and wait in it.

Twenty-Six

Every vein in Julian's body surged with panic, long after the fall. He had tried to calm down. In the car, in the waiting room, in the doctor's office, and now on the ride home, he had tried to calm down. He couldn't.

Nora still wouldn't look at him. She worried at her lip as they sat in the darkness, harsh headlights and streetlamps their only slivers of illumination. It would have been easier if he couldn't see her at all.

She drove home slowly. The roads were icy and lined miserably with sludge, though quiet for a Sunday night. He watched the Christmas lights dance across the window so he wouldn't have to look at her anymore. It didn't help. He still felt her body rise and fall with her quiet sighs, still saw the cogs in her brain raging, as his were.

Finally, when they came to a stop, he broke his silence with a cracked and brittle voice. "The doctor said it's a minor sprain. I should be on my feet again in two weeks." It felt pathetic to say after the fuss he had caused in the studio over it, but these feet were his only lifeline. Without them, he would be a mechanic working for his father in this dead-end town for the rest of his life. This was his way out, and that night, it might very well have been dashed.

"We have just over three until the show-case," Nora replied, her voice hollow as she turned onto his street. His small apartment complex was bathed in shadows, no lights flooding out of the windows, save for the hallway ones. He didn't want to go in there, didn't want to be left alone to think and worry.

"Then it's going to be a tough final week," he whispered as she parked. "Clear your schedule."

"And until then?"

Julian sighed, pinching the bridge of his nose as his eyelids shuttered. His head ached. His ankle ached. *He* ached. "Until then, I can still walk through the moves with you. Figure out any last-minute tweaks. I'll do what I can."

"Okay." She gave a terse nod, eyes fixed on the view in front of her.

"Were you hoping to get out of it?" He had intended to lift the mood with a joke, but it came out without any amusement.

"Yes, Julian," she ground out, raking her hand through her hair. It had fallen out of its ponytail at some point and hung loosely across her shoulders. Julian tried not to think of the way he had grasped that hair last night as she drove him to release. So much had changed in twenty-four hours. So much had been lost. "I intention-ally sabotaged you and put everything we did these last couple of months to complete waste. You foiled my cunning plan."

He knew deep down Nora would never do that. He had accused her of those things in the heat of the moment, when everything had fallen around him at once and pain carved through him with its blade. She was not that person. She was not vengeful or spiteful. She was stubborn and witty, all to hide that soft, caring heart he had glimpsed last night and this morning. Even after the fall she had taken care of him as he yelled at her. She had signed him in, brought him a stool to keep his ankle elevated as they waited, and helped him hop to the car without getting his bandages wet on the ground.

But she had still got him here. For whatever reason, she had lost focus and let this happen. He couldn't put his pride aside enough to apologize for the things he had said, the accusations he had made, though he knew well enough they were wrong. He had been distracted, too — because of her.

It didn't seem as though she expected any further conversation. She gripped the steering wheel tightly, face all thin lines.

"I'll see you tomorrow afternoon," was all he could utter out as he unclipped his seat belt.

"Need help getting inside?"

He almost winced at the offer. He didn't deserve it. "No. I'm good."

She said nothing. He was glad. Another

word might have kept him in that car all night.

Instead, he limped out and tried to ignore the icy shards of her gaze cutting like relentless hailstone down his back.

Twenty-Seven

It took a week for Julian to walk without searing pain burning through his ankle. It took another week for him to dance, and even then, he had to be careful. He didn't dare leap or do lifts again yet. Time was closing in on him, he breathed less easily with every passing second.

What made it worse was that he and Nora were barely talking. Even when they had still hated each other, they taunted and joked, but after the accident, they only discussed the choreography. He found out more from Fraser's rundown of his own lessons than from Nora himself — and he, apparently, had also noticed Nora's detachment.

He should have apologized, but she hadn't said anything, either. Why the hell, he wondered, should he be the first to say he was sorry when he was the one injured? She had been careless. If she couldn't admit that, he sure as hell didn't have to admit to his own mistakes, so they carried on with silent rehearsals until it drove him mad.

He was just about ready to fix it, but she had left early before he could even try, so he vowed to himself that he would try his own attempt at an apology the next day. He also vowed to her that he would join in properly again, no more walk-throughs or counterproductive practices, so she told him to rest his foot and meet her in the studio again in the morning.

He had agreed willingly, if only to rid himself of the unease that came with her these days, but he hadn't left after her. Instead, he stared at his reflection numbly. Nothing felt right anymore. Even the idea of getting into Phoenix didn't drive him the way it used to. He hadn't just lost his dance partner; he had lost his friend and whatever else Nora had become that still made him tingle with foreign feelings, and he wanted it back.

He hadn't known Constance was in her office until she wandered out at ten o' clock on the dot, tired bags dragging under her eyes. Julian hadn't seen her in a while, her pale, frail frame was a shock.

"Mr. Walker," she greeted him with a pleasant nod. That anything about her seemed pleasant was bizarre to Julian, but he returned it nonetheless and pretended as though he was being productive by weaving his wary feet across the floor.

"Miss Cassidy." He forced out a tight smile, cracking his knuckles against his palm uncomfortably.

"I see you're back on your feet."

"I am," he confirmed. "Luckily, it was only a sprain."

"Very lucky," she noted, with no hint of enthusiasm or concern. "Are you all set for the show-case? Costumes, music, etc.?"

"We're good to go." It was true: After seeing Nora in that oversize shirt the morning that felt eons ago now, he had ordered loose-fitting white shirts and black shorts for the both of them. It was simplistic — boring, perhaps — but it fit with the story they had created. Their bodies would do the heavy lifting.

Constance sighed. For the first time, Julian glimpsed pieces of Nora in the older woman — the way she huffed when something was left unsaid and the corners of her mouth drew down mor-osely. "I suppose Nora has told you the news."

"News?" Julian questioned, brows drawing together.

"Of my illness," she replied. "I am not a fool, Mr. Walker. The two of you are close. You do not have to pretend otherwise for my benefit. If any-thing, I am glad she has someone to confide in."

Julian faltered, shock draining the blood from his face. Illness? What did that even mean? "I'm sorry, Miss Cassidy. I haven't spoken to Nora about it. I had no idea."

Surprise flitted across her face. "Oh. I as-sumed...."

It didn't change anything. Perhaps he should have felt guilty for confronting Constance in the office that day, but it made no difference. She was still cruel and callous, still the woman who had tried to tear Nora apart. "It must be serious, if it's the reason you're retiring."

Constance shrugged and feigned nonchalance, but Julian caught the fear and exhaustion in her eyes. "We'll see."

It made sense now. If she had told Nora that Sunday, it was no wonder she had been withdrawn in the rehearsal afterwards. He could only imagine how brutal the conversation must have been and what it was doing to her to face losing another parental figure after her father, even if Constance hardly deserved the grief.

He was a fool. Nora had been grappling with this, and he had been too caught up in himself, in his need to get into Phoenix, to even notice that it wasn't about him. His heart ached for her.

Without thinking about it, he slipped on his jacket and shoes — no mean feat, with his ankle still supported with bandages. "I'm sorry to hear about your illness, Constance. Really, I am. But I have to go."

She waved a dismissive hand. "It's late. I was heading out myself. Goodnight, Mr. Walker."

Julian was already a foot through the threshold when he turned back and said, "Goodnight, Miss Cassidy."

He didn't walk with her to the parking lot. He was already being tugged to his car, to her, the door swinging shut behind him.

He had to talk to Nora. He had to make things right.

Twenty-Eight

The last thing Nora wanted that night was to be alerted of a visitor at ten-thirty. She was already in her fleeciest pajamas, fingers curled around a mug of cinnamon tea, her apartment lit only by the Christmas lights she had strung up last week to brighten her spirits.

It hadn't worked.

She huffed and peeked out the window. A shadow stood on the street, black and incongruous against the blanket of white that had fallen without her realizing. Still, she would know that stance and those broad shoulders anywhere.

Julian.

His silhouette pointed to her car. On the windshield, written in the snow in block capitals, were the words: *WE SHOULD TALK.*

Anxiety sunk like a stone in her stomach, she pulled away from the window wearily before buzzing him up. She took the few seconds it took him to ascend the narrow stairwell to collect herself, gulping down a few deep breaths with her back to the wall and clutching the warm mug to her chest. She didn't dare imagine what her hair, just washed and left to dry in untamed curls, looked like and tried not to think about the cartoonish snowflakes on her pants and penguins on her slippers.

She didn't have time to change now. His knock was harsh on the wood, it made her jump. She counted to five in her head before opening it.

Julian's hair was damp from the snow, flakes still dusting his shoulders. His cheeks were flushed from the cold, his lips chapped, dry, and pressed into a stern line that Nora didn't like the look of. She kept herself planted in the doorway, unwilling to let him in before she knew why he was there.

"What was it that couldn't have waited until tomorrow?" she questioned. "Don't tell me you forgot to buy the costumes."

"I have the costumes," he replied, as deadpan as he had been these last couple of weeks. It had been heartwrenching, not talking to him, not being able to apologize or fix things. But what she had done was past fixing, and what he had accused her of… she still couldn't wipe it from her mind. "I talked to Constance after you left the studio."

Nora nearly swore. What trouble had she caused now? "And?"

"She told me, Nora." His voice thawed, it made her own knees wobble in response. "She told me she's ill."

Nora's breath hitched. It wasn't like Constance to broadcast her ailments, but then, Constance was not herself these days. Still, Nora hadn't been prepared for this. She had been trying — and failing — to wipe it from her mind along with everything else. "Okay," she breathed finally. "And?"

"And…" He sucked in a breath, his eyes fluttering closed. When he opened them, they set on her with piercing determination that made her want to cower, to hide. "I had no idea. That day, in the studio… that was why you were so… that was why," he settled on.

"I was trying to make sense of it." It was an effort just to speak without letting the tears spill or her voice crack. "I still am."

"You could have told me."

Nora shook her head and shrugged. "Well, I didn't. What difference does it make?"

"It makes all the difference."

"Why? Because you feel sorry for me now?" she bit back, glowering at the very idea.

"Because you had just found out your grandmother was sick," he replied. "You were distracted. We both were. That was why it went wrong."

Nora couldn't help but sneer. "No, Julian, it went wrong because I was on some quest for vengeance, remember?"

"You know I didn't mean that." The muscles in his jaw hardened, eyes near black in the dim light. "I was angry and in pain and I made a mistake."

"Yes, you did," she agreed, "because if you

knew me—"

He cut her words off with her own. "I know you, Nora. I know you would never hurt anyone like that. You're not... you're not like me or Constance or anyone else who's ever done you wrong. I know that. I've always known that."

Nora swallowed down the bile in her throat and searched desperately for the anger that had lit within her only a second ago. It had ebbed just as quickly, chased away by the tenderness in his voice. She cast her eyes down to her slippers. "What do you want, Julian?"

"I came," he whispered through clenched teeth, "to say I'm sorry. I'm sorry, Nora. I'm so sorry. I've been wanting to apologize for the last two weeks, but as you love to remind me, I'm an arrogant bastard, and I wanted you to have to do it first."

Disbelief made her scoff. "I'm sorry I didn't play by your rules."

"You know that's not what I meant," he said. She was going to break if she looked at him. She felt fragile and small — meek, he had said once. After all this time, Julian Walker still had the power to unravel her and everything she thought she knew about herself. She hated him for it. She loved him for it.

"I miss you," he continued. "I miss you nagging me when I'm late, and I miss you poking fun at everything I say. I miss arguing with you, and I miss laughing with you. I miss that night we had together. I miss dancing with you the way we used to before I ruined everything. I miss everything, Nora, and I can't stand the thought of this going on another minute. I don't want to lose you."

"You won't even be here this time next month." Her words were a feeble attempt to protect herself, but they didn't work. The vulnerability in them was raw to her own ears.

"I won't be gone forever." He said it as though it was simple. Easy. Nothing between them had ever been those things, yet she wanted to believe him, to give in. "It's going to take more than a few months away to get rid of me, Cassidy."

She glanced up at him beneath her lashes in surprise. He hadn't called her that in so long. She had hated the nickname once, when it had been said with cockiness and dealt alongside verbal blows. Now, it meant they were *them* again. It meant they were going to be okay.

"I'm sorry," she spoke finally. "I never meant for you to get hurt."

"I know that," he murmured. "I never meant to hurt you, either. Now or any time before that."

He had proven that more than enough, even if she had been too blind to see it. He was not the boy who had dropped her off the stage, and she was not the girl who had fallen and quit. They were not teenagers anymore, and they didn't hate each other the way they once had.

"How did it get this messy?" It was a question she had posed to herself over and over again since Julian's fall.

Ever so slowly, Julian's cold hands found her face and cupped it. His pointer finger was red and frozen from the words he had written in the snow, dirt had gathered in crescent moons beneath the rough white tips of his nails. Goosebumps rose on Nora's skin in reaction to his touch, but she didn't shy away. "We can still fix it. Let me fix it. Please. Have I mentioned that I like your pajamas?"

Nora gulped down her tears and closed her eyes. "You caught me off guard." She shook her head and looked down at her nightwear. "You're always doing that."

"I do my best." His own mouth lifted into a crooked grin, flashing his white teeth. "So what now, Cassidy? Do you think you can forgive me?"

Nora pondered the question deliberately. He had hurt her. He would probably hurt her again. But he had also come here with apologies written all over his face, and she could not pretend she didn't see them. She had been miserable these past few weeks without him. She couldn't push him away forever.

"I'll think about it."

Julian sighed and planted a gentle kiss on her forehead. "Now?"

She hummed and sunk closer to him instinctively. She had missed him so badly, it left her numb.

Her response earned another peck, this time on her nose.

"Now?"

"Maybe."

Her jaw. Her hairline. Her knuckles. He grazed his lips across any inch of space he could reach, pleading for her forgiveness. In each of those kisses, she felt his regret, could identify it with ease because it lived beneath her flesh, too. Seeing him injured and lost and panicked because of her own carelessness had torn her apart. He had made his mistakes, and so had she.

She was tired of making the same ones, so when he finally found her mouth, she pulled him closer and rose on her tiptoes to reach him. Their kiss was delicate and slow and full of the apologies they had both been hiding from like cowards.

Still, she needed to be careful, so when he tried to deepen it, Nora pulled away to catch her breath. "I think we should wait until after the showcase."

"Right." Julian couldn't hide his disappointment, his hunger. It made her want to give in right away. "No distractions."

"I think we've well and truly broken that rule."

"More times than we can count," he agreed. He bowed his head once more to plant his final kiss, and she melted into him until she was dizzy. God, she had missed him. "Are you okay, Nora? With Constance?"

Something in her chest splintered. She'd been unable to talk about it with anyone but

Annie, and it had been eating away at her, especially when their rehearsals had been so silent. "I don't know," she answered honestly, "but I will be."

Pride seized his features. "Yes. You will."

When he said it, she knew it was true. She was about to finally ask him to come in when he pulled away.

"I'll see you tomorrow, then."

"Tomorrow." It was more than just a promise to see him. It was a promise that things were right again.

She watched Julian leave, no longer a limp in his step, and the heaviness that had been weighing on her chest the last few weeks finally lifted an inch.

She could breathe again.

Twenty-Nine

The final week had flown by without warning. Between rehearsals, Nora's lessons, and Julian's shifts at his father's repair shop, Nora and Julian had barely the time or energy to steal away the odd kiss, let alone figure out what they were to one another.

But then they were there. Everything they had worked for had arrived.

They walked into the auditorium hand in hand. Though it was only a small theater on the edge of town and nothing like the place where he had auditioned a couple of weeks ago, and though he had competed here thousands of times — one of them being the day he had dropped Nora — Julian marveled at the place nonetheless. In a few hours, people would be arriving to watch them. In a few hours, he would be burning beneath a spotlight with Nora.

The idea sent a surge of adrenaline through him so overpowering that he only noticed Nora's wide-eyed trepidation when he forced his eyes away from the stage to look down at her. "Ready for our last rehearsal?"

Nora swallowed with all the fear of a child,

it caused nerves to jitter in Julian's stomach. She was pale, exhaustion tugged on the edge of her features. "Is it too late to drop out?"

The attempt at a joke relieved Julian only slightly. He smirked anyway and gave her hand a reassuring squeeze. "Sorry, Cassidy. A deal's a deal."

Nora sucked in a ragged breath and pasted a courageous smile on her face. He had never admired her as much as he did now, watching her gulp down her anxiety for his benefit and seek out a bravery he could not even begin to comprehend. If she weren't here, he would have been a mess. Though he had been given the all clear, his ankle still didn't feel one-hundred percent, and combined with the pressure of finally achieving all he had ever dreamed of, that would have broken him under any other circumstances. But though the past week had been tiring, it had not been stressful. Nora had kept his stress at bay, always molding her time around him when he felt he needed to practice again, if only for the reassurance that they wouldn't mess this up.

Stupidly, he hadn't even realized until then that all of it would have such an effect on her. He hadn't realized that this place probably brought back memories she shouldn't have had to recall, yet she was the one who pulled him forward to the stage. She was the one to give him strength enough to do this — not just today, but all days.

Thirty

Nora had forgotten what it felt like to be this nervous. She had forgotten how it made her shiver, how it made her muscles spasm and her chest hammer. It was a miracle she had managed her makeup alone. With every second that went by, it got worse, until memories of the last time she had been here overwhelmed her.

He had dropped her. She had cried. Everyone had laughed. It had taken everything from her, this place, and she had let it. As she stared at her bone-white face in the mirror, she wasn't sure if she could retrieve it now. So many things could go wrong... and if any of them did, Julian would hate her guts. More than he used to. More than she had ever hated him.

She had to do this for him.

She combed through the tight curls she had set with enough hairspray to choke her to death — or tried, anyway. Her hands were trembling uncontrollably and it only made the brush snag and knot the hair even more. She set it down, inhaling through the tears threatening to spill any moment.

You're not that girl anymore, she repeated

to herself. *You're better than this now. Be brave. Be brave. Be brave.*

"Nora?" Julian appeared in the small mirror behind her, his face lined with worry as he eyed first her shaking hands and then her shattered expression.

He sat down on the stool next to her. She forced herself to smile at him, but it ended up more of a grimace, and then picked up the brush again. He pried it from her hands before she could try to tame it herself, as though he knew. As though he saw.

"I haven't..." She stammered over her words, and it only made her angry. *Be brave.* "I haven't done this since...."

"I know," he replied calmly, gently motioning for her to turn her head and dragging the teeth as carefully as he could through the tangles. "It's okay."

"It's not," she argued, voice thick as she reached that brink, where she felt she could no longer breathe, no longer move. How could she do this? How could she go out there? What if they remembered? What if they still saw her as that chubby girl who had no business being a contemporary dancer? "I'm a mess."

Be brave. She realized with a start that it wasn't her own voice willing her to gather her courage — it was her father's. She searched for him desperately across the white brickwork and untidy dressing room, as though she might find him standing over her.

She didn't, of course, but that didn't mean he wasn't there with her. It didn't mean she couldn't still make him proud.

"You're not a mess. You're nervous. That's okay. I'm nervous, too," he whispered, though the dressing room was otherwise empty. The show had already started, they had about twenty minutes before hordes of students rushed back from the several group dances Constance wanted to open with — to highlight the studio's camaraderie and diversity, she had said — while Nora and Julian waited in the wings. Nora was glad nobody else was there. She wasn't a teenager who could just fall apart in front of everyone. She was their teacher, too.

And heaven forbid Constance caught her in this state. She would most likely retract her offer to inherit the studio immediately.

Julian finished with her hair and she turned around, wiping the dampness from her bottom lids before her mascara could smudge. He offered her an encouraging smile, the pad of his thumb running soothing circles across her jaw and cheek, the corner of her mouth. "We're in this together now."

"What if I mess this up?" she questioned weakly.

"Then I'll mess it up with you," Julian shrugged, warm eyes creasing as he grinned. She kept her eyes locked on them, using them as her anchor, her way out of the deep tunnel she had been spiraling into before he had caught her and pulled her back to the surface. "It's just one dance."

"It's not." She shook her head. "It's everything. You need this."

"I don't need anything but you." The statement was so ridiculous she had to roll her eyes, but he forced her gaze back to him quickly. "I mean it, Nora. I want to get into Phoenix, but I want you more — regardless of what happens out on that stage."

"You're saying you'd forgive me if I fucked this up royally?" Her tone, so disbelieving, brought an amused laugh up from Julian's throat.

"You're not going to fuck this up. But yes, I'd forgive you. I'm sure you'd find a way to make it up to me if it came to that."

She shook her head and returned her focus to the mirror, chest heaving with shallow breaths.

"Deep breaths," he murmured, his hand warming the space between her shoulder blades. She wasn't even dressed yet and they only had ten minutes before they needed to be backstage, ready. *Ten minutes.*

Still, she obeyed and tried to steady herself with her head in her hands, concentrating on the weight of his touch and the quiet around them. A water bottle was placed in front of her a moment later. "Don't you dare go passing out on me, Cassidy. You're not getting out of this now."

She would have laughed, but all she could

do was let him unscrew the bottle cap, watching the faint tremor in his own fingers as he forced it to her lips. She sipped slowly, the cool liquid soothing her aching throat. *Be brave. Be brave. Be brave.*

"Just don't drop me again," she warned sternly when she was done.

"You know I won't." His fingers were all over her, grazing the hairs clinging to the nape of her neck, her shoulders, her spine, finding any place he could in an attempt to calm her down. It was working — slowly. "I'll never let you go. I'll fall with you if I have to, but I swear I won't let you go."

The fact that he wasn't completely riddled with nerves when this meant more to him than anything meant that she shouldn't have been, either. She had less to lose. Nothing that happened that night could have been much worse than what had happened last time.

She took a final breath and nodded. "Then I suppose I had better get dressed."

Julian grinned that dazzling, perfect grin she had grown to love and planted a soft kiss on her lips, overwhelming her so her nerves no longer could. "That's my girl," he whispered in her ear.

Nora's entire stomach flipped at just those three words, it was an effort to pull away from him and gather her composure.

Be brave, she demanded of herself a final time. This time, it was not her father's voice telling her to do so. It was her own.

∞∞∞

Julian had made the right choice with the costumes. Nora had been dreading the idea that he might put her in a floaty little dress or an awful nylon leotard and tights, but the plain white shirt that he also wore beside her set her at ease. The shirt slid off her shoulder on one side, and when she made the effort to pull it back up, Julian stopped her. "It looks better like that."

His eyes darkened and she knew what it meant. He still wanted her.

She could no longer see all of the things she used to hate about herself in her reflection. Once, all she'd ever done was curse her legs for being so thick and lumpy with cellulite and stretch marks. Now, she saw they were dancer's legs, strong and padded with muscle. The curve of her hips that she had always cursed for being so wide were hips that Julian had touched so lovingly. She was proud of them. She was proud of all of it.

She had been working so hard to prove she was not that girl who had fallen and cried and given up that day of the competition, but there was nothing left to prove, regardless of how the next ten minutes went. Nothing in the mirror was shattered or wrong. She had returned to the thing that broke her, and she would emerge victorious beside Julian. She imagined her seventeen-year-old self standing in awe beside her, admiring the woman she had become. She had chosen not to change, not to lose weight or run away from the studio. She had chosen second chances and bravery. She had chosen trust. She had chosen herself, without apologies or change. It had all been worth it.

The sound of cheers ricocheted through the echoing audience down the corridor. It was the last performance before theirs. They needed to go.

Still, Julian placed his strong hands on her shoulders and kissed the back of her head. "Ready?"

"Ready," she smiled shakily, turning into him and pressing her lips to his. The taste of him was enough to warm her soul and put her mind, finally, to rest. "Are you?"

"As I'll ever be. I'm glad it was you in the end, Cassidy," he murmured. "You're the only one I trust to do this with me. I wouldn't be here without you."

"Yes, you would," she responded gently. "You'd just be bored witless with a dance partner who actually likes you."

He laughed, breathing her in as his fingers twirled in her hair. She could suddenly feel his own anxiety, turning him rigid and keeping him hovering there, in the between — in the before. Everything would change when they went out on that stage… everything but them. She was certain of that, that whatever they were couldn't be touched by whatever awaited them. Phoenix. Constance. The stage and whatever was to happen on it.

Julian was steady as a rock. He had been since their first rehearsal. She knew him as well as she knew herself, could sense every movement he was to make before he made it, yet she could never have predicted what came out of his mouth next.

"I love you."

"Are you planning on dancing today, or is the dressing room more accommodating than the audience waiting for you to perform outside?" Constance's voice resonated like metal against metal, sounding out on almost the same beat as Julian's declaration.

Nora gulped down the emotion that rose in response, gulped down the fear and the longing and the love — because she felt it, too. She loved him, too.

But she didn't have the time or courage to tell him. Constance was waiting with a frosty expression, her face painted with rouge and pink lipstick and ice that had just barely begun to thaw.

"Well?" she asked when Nora drew her gaze away from Julian's strained expression.

"Well," she repeated nervously, taking Julian's hand in her own and shaking her feet as though the anxiety might fall straight out of them. "This is it."

Julian blew out a final breath and nodded. "This is it."

Thirty-One

The thin curtain was the last shred of armor Nora had, in a moment, she would be unveiled.

Julian's and Nora's hands swung, interlocked, in the space between them. They would have to let go in a moment. Nora tried not to think about what would happen when they did, instead drinking down the last dregs of his reassuring smile. He had her back. He wouldn't let her go this time.

"I got you, Cassidy." His quiet words confirmed it, an echo of one of their first rehearsals together. She had been so afraid then, afraid of him and herself and afraid to dance, to put herself on display again. To be vulnerable. Now, she felt ready, and the anticipation left her restless.

"I got you right back," she replied, because it had never been one-sided. She needed him to know that. She was here for him just as much as she was here for herself.

He cast her a final glance, one that held more meaning than she could begin to understand in her current state, then the first bar of music floated out from somewhere behind them, the spotlight burned through the curtain, it was time.

Their hands fell to their sides, and they danced.

It was just the two of them. The audience might as well not have been there. Nora didn't see them in the shadows of the auditorium. She saw only Julian, bathed in silver light. Radiant. Alive. Crashing into her.

They glided and hurtled, contracted and softened, froze and thawed, always together. They could have ripped the stage apart with their desperate feet if they wanted to.

They were tornados, greater and more life-wrecking still when they were pulled into one another over and over until they merged and became one big, undefeatable cyclone that tore through every splinter of the stage. Nora made every breath, every moment, every beat count, putting every slither of herself into the movements. There was no time to fall. Every motion rolled through her muscles without needing to be summoned, and Julian remained her pillar, her rock, their feet in a unison that could never be broken.

She wanted it to stay that way forever.

The fade of the music brought her back to herself. She ended on the floor, twisted across Julian after a struggle and then a reconciliation that told their story without them ever realizing it until then. The world turned black. Claps and cheers erupted and lifted something vital in Nora's chest. She had done it. She had made it through. She had not fallen or failed.

Julian gathered her up in his arms when the roar of the applause finally dulled. Delirious laughter bubbled from her as he pulled her back into the wings and swung her around before she had even the time to glimpse his face.

"We did it," he whispered elatedly into her ear. "We did it, Nora. It was perfect."

"Perfect" was not a word she had ever been offered before, but she didn't reject it then. Tears streamed down her face as she gasped desperately for breath. The stage had stolen it. *He* had stolen it.

With her legs wrapped around his hips, she cradled his jawline as he wiped away her tears. "I love you, too," she said finally, and though it was delayed, he seemed not to care.

The performance might have been over, but they weren't. Even now, they soared together, tangled together, leapt together as they kissed.

And Julian was right. It was perfect.

Thirty-Two

The theater's foyer brimmed with people, some faces Nora recognized, some she didn't. Jennifer Phoenix, wearing a wide, red lipstick grin, was one of the former.

Nora felt Julian tense against her as he spotted her, too, especially as the crowd shifted with praises sung to them out of thin air from people Nora did not have focus enough to have a conversation with. Her adrenaline was still sending her heart into a fit.

Constance stood with the director, lost in whatever it was they were talking about.

"Are your ears burning?" Nora questioned lightly, looking up at him. "They're probably talking about you."

"Do you think it was enough?"

She wanted to kiss away any hint of insecurity that passed across his features. Instead, she dragged him forward. "We'll soon find out."

Jennifer's face lit up when she noticed the two of them approaching. She held a champagne flute in her hand and even without it would easily be the most sophisticated and professional woman here, even beside Constance. Nora regretted only throwing a cardigan and pleated trousers on rather than changing into a dress.

"Here they are," she crooned as they reached her. "The dynamic duo, in the flesh. I was just telling Constance how utterly beautiful the dance was."

Julian's jaw locked and feathered, so Nora answered for him. "Thank you. We're grateful you came."

"I wouldn't have missed it." Her eyes were as warm and welcoming as Nora remembered the first time they had met and lingered on her as well as Julian. "The two of you are very talented. The way you feed off each other when you dance is not something I've seen in awhile. I'm impressed."

"To think there was a time you couldn't stand to be in the same room as one another," Constance added knowingly.

"Well, it took a lot of hard work," Nora beamed up at Julian as his arm snaked around her waist, "but we got there in the end."

"You certainly did." Jennifer nodded and placed her champagne on the front desk, clearing her throat. "But I think that's enough dancing around it. I know why I'm here, and so do you, Mr. Walker."

"Yes, ma'am." Julian bowed his head gravely. Nora gave his arm a squeeze of reassurance and felt the hard muscle tighten with tension.

Jennifer gave a clandestine smile, studying the two of them for a moment as she clasped her hands together. "You can breathe a sigh of relief. I've seen more than enough of your talent, and I would be honored to have you join the company."

The wind fell out of Julian and whispered through Nora's hair. He laughed in disbelief as Jennifer offered her hand out for him to shake. He took it a little too enthusiastically and nearly tore off a limb. Nora could do nothing but grin proudly at the interaction, trying not to think of what it would mean for them — that he would be leaving. It felt as though she had only just got him, after all.

"However, I have another proposition," Jennifer continued, her dark eyes flitting to Nora. Curiosity glittered there, and Nora shifted uneasily at the center of it. "It's quite clear to me that Mr. Walker isn't the only great talent in this theater. Miss Cassidy, you danced quite beautifully tonight."

It took Nora a moment to realize the compliment was directed at her and not her grandmother. She had never been "Miss Cassidy" before; that title was always reserved for Constance. "Thank you."

"I'd like to offer you a place in my company, too. I think you would make a great asset to my troupe."

Nora's brows furrowed in confusion. She glanced at Constance, who wore a proud yet wary smirk on her wrinkled lips — one that had never been directed at Nora before. Then, instinctively, her eyes fell to Julian. He was just as taken aback as she was, features cycling through shock, relief, excitement. It was enough to make her stomach flutter with a joy, an adoration, she had never felt so intensely before.

Her attention slid behind his tall frame, to her students. They were bustling with post-performance glee as their parents and friends showered them with praises and embraces. Many of them she had taught for years. Others she hadn't even begun to get to know yet. All of them were pieces of her, one way or another.

Dancing with Julian had been everything she had needed, but not for this. Not to return to performances. No, it had made her remember all of the things that dance should have been for her: an expression, a passion, an art. She loved it for that, but she loved passing that knowledge on more than anything. What would happen to the dance studio if she was not there when Constance retired? What would happen to Fraser? To all of the other children who hadn't always belonged and yet had still found something to love, somewhere to feel safe and fortified?

It was what she had always wanted. It was what she still wanted, perhaps more than ever. Julian belonged on the stage, and perhaps she did, too, but she also belonged in the studio. She wanted to nurture those children who felt like she once had. She wanted to be the teacher she wished she'd had growing up. She wanted to make a difference for others and not just herself.

"I'm completely taken aback and incredibly grateful for the offer," Nora breathed finally, "but I have to decline, Miss Phoenix. My place is here. These children need somebody to guide them, to accept them, to let them dance without worry. I want to be that person more than anything else."

She looked to Constance. Her face had smoothed with every word, the concern dissipating as quickly as it had come.

"I'm needed here," Nora continued, looking only at her grandmother. "And more than that, I want to be here."

"Are you certain?" Jennifer frowned. She was probably used to being the one to turn others down, rather than have her own offers declined. Nora did not feel any hesitance, though, as her eyes snapped back to the woman.

"Yes," Nora said unwaveringly. "I'm absolutely certain. Thank you, Miss Phoenix."

"If you change your mind, be sure to have Mr. Walker give you my contact details."

"Of course," Julian replied for her.

"I'll be seeing you in the new year, Julian."

Julian nodded, his eyebrows still knitted together as they both watched Jennifer disappear into the crowd. Before Nora could gauge Julian's feelings about all of it, Constance placed her hand on Nora's arm.

"I'm proud of you, child." It was the first time she had ever said it, the first time Nora had ever heard it. She could do nothing but gape, her heart both tearing and mending itself with the words she had always longed for. "You've come a long way."

Nora's eyes filled with tears.

"Your father would be proud, too. He would have loved to see you dance that way tonight."

"Thank you," Nora managed to choke out, squeezing Constance's hand lightly. As though it was quite enough emotion for one night, Constance ambled away to a group of parents in the corner, most likely ready to bask in their praises.

Nora was afraid to turn and face Julian, but she did. Bewilderment still creased his features. "You just turned down the opportunity of a life-time."

"Yes," Nora said. "I did."

"Why?" His eyes searched her, trying to grasp any explanation in her he could find.

"Because," her eyes flitted to Fraser, stand-ing with his mother on the edge of the crowd. "I meant what I said. Performing with you... it was everything, Julian, but it isn't my dream. The stu-dio is mine now, and I want more than anything to make sure no other child has to feel as unworthy and insecure as I felt growing up there. I want dance to be what it was always supposed to be: fun, accepting, liberating. I can't do that if I'm not here."

"And this is what you want?" he asked. "This isn't because Constance wants you to take over?"

"No," she assured him. "This was my decision. It's what I want. It's what I've always wanted."

It was clear some part of him was disappointed. She could have gone with him, danced with him a hundred times over. Instead, she was unintentionally cleaving them apart. Still, he nodded. He understood. "Then I'm proud of you. You're going to be the best thing that's ever happened to those kids."

"You think?"

"Well," he shrugged, eyes falling to his shoes. "You probably were for me. I can only imagine how much they'll love you, too."

"Probably?" She arched an eyebrow, falling into him with ease.

"Definitely," he amended wryly, his breath fanning across her face as he brushed the hair from her face. "So don't go thinking you're getting rid of me just because you'll be here and I'll be with Phoenix. I'll be back to annoy you all the time, Cassidy."

"You don't have to be in the same town as me to do that," she quipped. "I can bicker with you just as easily over the phone."

"Still." His voice fell to an amused, gravely cadence that made her toes curl. "It's not the same if I can't see you rolling your eyes at me."

Nora hummed, tracing circles into his collarbone absently. "I suppose it might be good to remind myself of that annoying, arrogant smirk every once in a while."

"There are children in the room," a voice chided from behind them.

Nora pulled out of Julian's arms reluctantly and turned to find Julian's mother standing before them, Fraser beside her. She was smiling despite her words, though Fraser looked uncomfortable enough for the both of them.

"Mom!" Julian pulled his mother into a hug and then patted Fraser in greeting. Nora couldn't help but admire the way he softened and the corners of his eyes creased with love. "I'm glad you both came."

"So?" she urged. "What's the verdict? Are you leaving us?"

"I'm not leaving anybody," Julian denied, causing Nora to roll her eyes. "But I did get into Phoenix."

His mother immediately teared up with pride. She was just like him, her skin a soft, dewy brown and her hair tousled with curls. She even had the same dimples and almond eyes. Where his father was all of the stern, harsh lines of his face, this woman was all of his beauty and grace. Nora could see that without having to look very hard.

"I'm so proud of you, Julian," she fussed, hugging him again. "So proud."

Julian's face hardened. "I invited Dad tonight. Did he come?"

His mother shook her head apologetically.

He had told Nora about the invite yesterday, that he thought perhaps if his father watched him dance just once, he might understand why it mattered so much. Nora despised Graham for letting him down that way. It made her realize how lucky she had been to have her own caring father, if only for a short time. Still, it was clear how much his mother and brother adored him — and she did, too. He didn't need Graham.

"It doesn't matter, sweetheart." His mother cupped Julian's cheek. "You followed your heart. Even with him tearing you down, you did what you love unapologetically. Not seeing you, not cheering you on… that's his loss."

"I know."

Nora felt Fraser's guarded eyes on her. "Are you leaving, too?"

"Leaving *you*?" Nora ruffled Fraser's wild hair gently. "I couldn't do that, could I?"

Fraser's mouth curled into a glimmer of a smile, more than she had ever earned from him before. She had endless love and care for the young boy in whom she saw so much of herself. He was too young to be so wary of this world. She only prayed she could help him through whatever other struggles he had yet to bear, whether that be in the studio or out of it.

"Well, you'll definitely be seeing more of Fraser in the new year," his mother chimed in, casting Nora a warm, beautiful grin that reminded her so much of Julian's. "He's asked if he can join a few more classes."

"What about Dad?" Julian asked.

"Until that man knows how to be a father, he won't have a say in Fraser's life anymore. I think we've all dealt with him for long enough, don't you?"

The words caused Julian to slump with what Nora could only assume to be relief. *Good*, she thought. They were all better off without him.

It was then that a familiar couple caught Nora's eye at the other end of the foyer. Annie and Meg were waiting patiently for Nora to notice them, they waved as soon as her eyes fell to them. Nora lit up and waved back, excusing herself quickly.

"Wait," Julian held her back by the wrist. "Meet me back in there later?" He motioned with his head to the auditorium.

Nora frowned but nodded, her eyes fluttering shut as he planted a quick kiss to her forehead before letting her go.

Annie and Meg had clearly watched the whole thing because they crooned like children as Nora made her way over to them.

"So *that's* the reason you left our wedding early," Annie accused. "And I suppose I won't be expecting you at the café anymore?"

Nora cast Annie an apologetic glance as she enveloped her tightly, pulling Meg in, too. "Do I have to hand in a resignation and my apron?" She had still been working the odd shift when she'd had the time, but she had seen less and less of Annie these last few weeks, especially as they drew closer to the show. She wasn't sure she'd have any time at all to work there in the new year.

"Nah," Annie dismissed nonchalantly with a wave of her hand. "As long as you still come in as a customer every now and again. Keep the apron as a parting gift."

"You'll be seeing me plenty, I'm sure."

"You were wonderful up there, Nora."

"Really wonderful," Meg agreed, linking her arm through Annie's. "We always knew you would be, though."

"And it looks like Julian thought so, too." Annie wiggled her eyebrows suggestively. "I won't be needed to threaten him and his balls again, will I?"

Nora chuckled and glanced longingly over at Julian. He was a head taller than everyone else and still stood with his family, wearing a divinely content grin that warmed Nora. She hoped he never lost that grin. She loved that grin.

She loved him.

"Save it for now. I'll let you know if I need your assistance."

"You'd better," Meg threatened with a nudge.

Annie was already yawning and it occurred to Nora that it was probably getting late. She felt bad for keeping them waiting this long, so wrapped up in everything else that happened in so little time. She could already imagine how it would feel lying in bed tonight, wondering how any of it was real.

Would Julian be beside her?

"Well, we have an early start at the café tomorrow, but we wanted to come and cheer you on," Annie said finally, checking her wristwatch before hugging Nora again.

Nora nestled into her shoulder appreciatively. "Thank you so much for coming."

"Of course." Her gloved hand rubbed her back in comfort. "I'll see you on Christmas Day?"

Nora nodded and pulled away. It was tradition to spend Christmas with Annie, Meg, and their small circle of family, since she had never had a family of her own. "Of course. See you later."

Annie and Meg cast her waves of goodbye before weaving their way toward the door. Nora couldn't suppress her smile as she stood back and took in the foyer. It teemed with an excitement she hadn't felt in a long time, though it had emptied slowly as she'd been talking.

She had missed this buzz. She had missed the satisfaction, pride, and adrenaline. She had missed dancing, and she had missed *loving* dance. She had said once that dance had abandoned her, but she knew then that it hadn't — and she hadn't abandoned it, either. It had always lived in her and always would.

It was time to stop hiding from it.

Thirty-Three

It was eerie, walking into the auditorium once it was void of life again, knowing that it had been electric with applause and music only an hour or two ago. Julian waited for her beneath the spotlight, the rest of the room shrouded in blackness, the seats folded up and programs scattered across the aisles. The curtain they'd used as their most beloved prop still hung from above, the silk rippling behind Julian in a phantom breeze.

Oddly, she felt almost as nervous as she had before going on stage, the only difference being that there was no longer anything to fear and everything to look forward to.

He paced, burning a hole into the stage with the soles of his feet, but he stopped when she began to take the steps up onto the platform. She squinted as she came into the light, aware that he watched her every move as though they were still dancing.

Their eyes locked. He smiled, shadows kissing the sharp hollows of his cheeks and fragmenting his face into a hundred separate shards of light and dark.

"I can't believe it's over," she said. "We made

it here. Finally."

He nodded and looked out into the auditorium as though the audience still sat there, watching. This was not a performance, though. She could see that in the intensity of his gaze, the way his dark eyes pierced through her when he finally came close enough to touch.

"Don't sound too happy about it."

Nora snorted. "I can't help it. I've been waiting years to finally bid you goodbye."

His mouth uncoiled into a dangerous smirk. He pulled her close with a force she hadn't felt before and her breath caught against the crashing of rib cages. "If you wanted that, Cassidy, you shouldn't have made me fall for you."

"Can't help it," she whispered breathlessly. "It's my natural charm."

He rested his forehead against hers as though she was his lifeline, eyes flitting down to her lips so she could see every dark lash curling against his high cheekbones.

"Tell me this won't end." The desperate plea shocked her enough that she faltered, and if it wasn't for his steady arms braced against her back, she might have collapsed altogether. "Tell me we'll be together even when we're apart."

"Julian," she murmured delicately, and there was no hiding the love that swelled in the way she said his name. "I'm not lucky enough to be rid of you, remember?"

"Nora." He was begging her to stop joking. He was begging for her to be real. Her heart wrenched at the fact.

"It won't end," she vowed. "We'll be okay. We're always okay, even when we're not."

It was enough for him to ease around her and she melted into him as he finally gave her the thing she craved most. He kissed her as he never had before, it reverberated through her every bone and every fiber. She loved him. She loved him. She loved him.

And it wouldn't end. This cemented it more than words ever could.

"I'll never forget how it felt, dancing with you tonight." Even as he said it, he swayed to an invisible tune, his hips rolling against hers.

"Me, neither."

"Do it again with me, one last time."

Nora frowned, pressing her hands to his chest so that she could better look at him. "Now? Here?"

"Have you got somewhere else to be tonight, Cassidy?" he questioned, the confidence returning to his voice. "Am I keeping you?"

"Actually, I have a hot date waiting outside."

"Better tell them to go. I have other plans for us." He paused before requesting again, "Dance with me."

She rolled her eyes but couldn't suppress her smirk. "The duet?"

"No," he said. "Let's improvise. Just dance with me."

"There's no music," Nora pointed out.

Julian sighed as though the statement caused him unnecessary hassle but pulled his phone out of his pocket anyway, the screen illuminating his face. A moment later, a piano-heavy melody played out with no lyrics and he set it down on the edge of the stage.

"You're a hard woman to please."

"I challenge you, remember?" she retorted, sarcasm dripping from every syllable as she used his own words against him. Still, she watched as he got a feel for the new music and began to move around her, gauging the right moment to join in. It was difficult. She loved watching the way his body moved, rippling and contracting with jerks and then smooth transitions a moment later. Like tidal waves. She would have been happy letting him go at it alone, but when he grabbed her hand, she knew she had no choice.

How strange it was that she had once flinched from that touch, that they had ever been anything but this: them. Now, she was more comfortable with his skin against hers than she ever thought possible. He made her feel safe and wanted. He wrapped her up and lifted her effortlessly.

Though it felt like home, it still terrified her.

Be brave, said a voice floating above the music, and she knew the words were no longer meant for dancing or performing. They were made for him.

She had fallen once because of Julian Walker, and it had ruined everything, and there she was again. Falling. She wouldn't fight it. She wouldn't run.

She would let him catch her, like he always seemed to now.

She would do what they did best. She would dance with him until the music faded and her heart stopped beating.

They would both do it, and they would do it, this time, together.

Epilogue

The new year had brought with it a swarm of new students that Nora had not been expecting. Almost every open session she taught that first day was full, and the sign-up sheet for private lessons was already scrawled with ink by three o' clock that afternoon.

It was busy and tiring and it was only the beginning of it all, but she didn't mind. When the schools went back from Christmas break, it would be quieter, she told herself.

Constance was still hovering around, unwilling to let the studio go quite yet, though she had started her new treatment just the week before and Nora could tell she was attempting to take a step back. Truth be told, Nora didn't mind her presence. She was glad — proud, even — that Constance was here to witness the success of her first day. Besides, it wouldn't have felt right without her. She would always be a significant part of this dance studio, just as her father still was.

Nora could feel him even then, as she wished the final class of the day a goodbye. He was guarding this place and her. Smiling, probably, because she had finally found her own purpose in the world.

She offered him a secret smile to the ceiling when Constance finally retired to her office — the office that was soon to be Nora's. She had already begun coaching her in all of the business jargon, the spreadsheets and finances and all of the other things that Nora had a hard time understanding. Still, she tried not to let it go over her head. She wanted this to work more than anything.

Well, almost anything.

Julian knew her schedule better than she did, he sauntered in at five on the dot. It was strange to see him in something other than his usual dancewear in this place, but there he stood, wearing jeans and a shirt with the top few buttons loose. *Good.* It would save Nora time later.

It was their last night. She pushed down the sadness that welled in her as she hugged him, the scent of his cologne wrapping around her and making her dizzy.

"How did it go?"

"Perfect," she beamed. "Most of the classes were full and I got plenty of sign-ups for private lessons."

"Everyone wants a one-on-one with Nora Cassidy." Pride made his chest swell. "I can hardly blame them. I suppose I can't keep you all to myself anymore."

"Nope," she grinned. "They all sang your praises, though. A few of them were at the showcase."

"I expect fifty percent of the profit, then, if I'm the one getting them through the door."

Nora smacked his chest, only now noticing the bag slung across his shoulder. "What's this?"

A sly smirk curled on his features as he put the bag down and unzipped it to reveal what lay inside. From what Nora could see, it was nothing but a few blankets. "I wanted our last night to be special. So..." He pulled out the blankets and lay them on the floor, leaving Tupperware filled with food and a bottle of wine visible at the bottom of the bag. Nora's heart fluttered. "I figured, why not stay here for a while tonight?"

"You want to have our last date before you leave me for three months in the studio?" Nora wrinkled her nose, accepting the wine glass he thrust into her hand. They had already arranged his next visit, since he had received his schedule from Phoenix late the week before. Rehearsals would be full-on for a while, but he had a long weekend free in March, and Nora had offered to drive up to London to see him when she could, too, though it would be difficult when she was teaching so much.

Still, she had already planned to hire a few other teachers if she earned enough profit, and there were already two others that had helped Constance out for years. She wouldn't be doing this alone. She had faith that the long distance would be enough for them, even if she would miss him with every stutter of her heart.

"This is where it all started for us," he answered softly, the wine glugging as he poured it first into her glass and then his own. "Maybe you shouldn't have taken down the Christmas lights yet. We're lacking the ambience."

Nora scoffed in amusement and placed her glass down before heading to the light controls beside the stereo. A disco ball had been installed decades ago, when freestyle dancing had been more popular than contemporary and lyrical. It hadn't been used for years, but tonight, it would come in handy.

She turned it on and spots of light floated around the room as though they were sitting inside a kaleidoscope. It wasn't quite as beautiful as the fairy lights, but it sufficed when she turned the main lights off and the twirling disco ball worked its outdated magic.

"Very suave," Julian commended her as he sat and pulled out paper plates.

"Don't get any food on the floor," she ordered as she joined him. "Constance will kill me."

"Well, unfortunately, Miss Cassidy, Constance can do no such thing." He opened the box to reveal spaghetti. In the other, cheesy garlic bread. Nora's favourite, he had learned not so long ago. "This is your studio now, remember?"

A content sigh escaped Nora as she scanned her surroundings. It didn't feel like hers quite yet, but it would soon enough. "I keep forgetting."

"Then I'll just have to keep reminding you."

He spooned out the spaghetti onto paper plates, the Bolognese sauce a sharp and comforting scent that made her forget where they were for a moment. "So romantic."

"I do my best." Julian sucked the excess sauce from his fingers before serving the garlic bread, too. Nora could only watch him in awe. She still found it difficult to believe he was hers and she his. After everything she had accomplished the past year — returning to performing and learning to love herself through it, choreographing a duet, inheriting the studio — Julian Walker had been the biggest surprise of all.

She didn't want him to leave her, but she was so proud of him for going. She knew what Phoenix meant to him, just as he knew what the studio meant to her. She could only pray that somewhere between this small town and London, they could find their common ground and make it work.

Julian's brows drew together as he noticed her staring. "What's ticking in that brain of yours, Cassidy?"

"Just thinking about how far we've come," she admitted, sipping her wine and stretching her tired legs out in front of her on the blankets. "If you would have told me last year that I'd be sitting in my own dance studio having dinner with Julian Walker, I would have laughed in your face."

"Laughed in my face?" he repeated. "You're

not nearly that polite. You probably would have spat out your usual spiel about how much of an arrogant bastard I am."

Nora laughed at the accuracy. "And then the rest."

He joined in, gazing at her so fixedly she might have collapsed then and there. "We really did make it, didn't we?"

"Yes, we did." She softened, leaning forward so she could reach for him. He met her in the middle and kissed her for long enough that he might have been making up for all of the times they were about to lose when he left tomorrow. It made her stomach writhe and shudder with pleasure, love, and desire — and sadness, because soon, he would be gone.

Julian's expression turned solemn when she finally pulled away. "I'm going to miss being able to do that anytime I want."

"Then make the most of it now," she begged.

His eyes glittered as a spot of light passed over him. "I have a few other ideas of how we can spend tonight."

"Is that right?" Flames ignited in her belly as his knuckles grazed her waist.

Julian hummed, standing and offering her his hand. She already knew what he was going to ask.

"Dance with me again, Nora Cassidy."

Though she was tired from a hectic day, her feet throbbed from being on them for hours on end, and she was starving for more than just the food laid out in front of her, Nora stood and took Julian's hand.

He pulled her in close and she wondered how on Earth she could ever let him go now. She pushed the dread away as he spun her without warning, the way he always loved to do.

This studio was their home, their shelter, their life source, and tonight — and, Nora hoped, many more nights after — it was filled with their laughter and their hope for a future they had only once been able to dream of. A future that, one day, might be spent together.

They would dance for that future until they were breathless, as if the spots of light orbiting them were planets and they the scorching Sun at the center of it all — where they should be. Where they had always been. Where their souls would always be, even when their bodies weren't.

They had built their home there, together. In Julian's arms, Nora was absolutely certain it would not crumble.

About The Author

Rachel Bowdler

Rachel Bowdler is a freelance writer, editor, and sometimes photographer from the UK. She spends most of her time away with the faeries. When she is not putting off writing by scrolling through Twitter and binge-watching sitcoms, you can find her walking her dog, painting, and passionately crying about her favourite fictional characters. You can find her on Twitter and Instagram @rach_bowdler.

Books By This Author

The Fate Of Us

A Haunting At Hartwell Hall

Handmade With Love

Partners In Crime

Paint Me Yours

Safe And Sound

Saving The Star

The Secret Weapon

Printed in Great Britain
by Amazon

72238432R00151